I0525295

Liv and Breathe

by

Misty Simon

This is a work of fiction. Names, characters, places, and incidents are either the product of the author's imagination or are used fictitiously, and any resemblance to actual persons living or dead, business establishments, events, or locales, is entirely coincidental.

Liv and Breathe

COPYRIGHT © 2019 by Misty Simon

All rights reserved. No part of this book may be used or reproduced in any manner whatsoever without written permission of the author or The Wild Rose Press, Inc. except in the case of brief quotations embodied in critical articles or reviews.
Contact Information: info@thewildrosepress.com

Cover Art by *Debbie Taylor*

The Wild Rose Press, Inc.
PO Box 708
Adams Basin, NY 14410-0708
Visit us at www.thewildrosepress.com

Publishing History
First Champagne Rose Edition, 2019
Print ISBN 978-1-5092-2485-2
Digital ISBN 978-1-5092-2486-9

Published in the United States of America

She might as well take a chance and tell her side before Mr. High and Mighty came rolling into town—if he could unglue himself from his society life long enough to take any interest.

"Some boys in town say they saw my boys over in Beckham's pastures trying to tip over cows. When these town kids came along, they said they spooked the camp boys, who took off running. According to the accusers, that's how the fence was broken and how the alpacas got out and ran away. Beckham still hasn't found two of them."

By this time, there was a solid crowd of about twenty people hemming Liv and Betty in at the counter. As much as Liv appreciated the looks of outrage for her camp boys, and for the situation in general, she didn't blame the Beckhams for pressing charges. Especially with the graffiti Mr. Beckham had told her was spray-painted on the side of his barn.

She just couldn't wrap her head around the idea that her boys would do something so destructive when they knew the consequences and the punishment for not toeing the line.

"I don't believe it," Betty declared, and had the majority of the other people agreeing with her both verbally and by nodding their heads. "There's no way the boys at Breathe would jeopardize their time here by doing something so stupid."

Liv would have said the same thing to her boss, Alex Campbell, this morning if he'd picked up his phone.

Praise for Misty Simon and...

POISON IVY:
"I loved this book...laughing during most of it."
~*Rae, My Book Addiction and More (4.5)*
~*~

THE WRONG DRAWERS:
"...a sass filled, one-two punch of delightfully quirky humor and intriguing mystery."
~*Jacki King, bestselling author*
~*~

WHAT'S LIFE WITHOUT THE SPRINKLES?:
"...has warmth, her characters seem like real people, and her plotting drew me in..."
~*Angie Just Read, The Romance Reviews*
~

"If you enjoy romance stories about two people burned by relationships gone bad...then look no further."
~*Xeranthemum, Long and Short Reviews (4.5 Books)*
~*~

Dedication

To all the staff at TWRP,
you have made my dreams come true
and I will never be able to thank you enough!

Misty Simon's books at The Wild Rose Press

The Kissinger Kisses Series
What's Life Without the Sprinkles?
Making Room at the Inn
Go Ahead, Make My Bouquet
Christmas in Kissinger

~

The Ivy Morris Mysteries
Poison Ivy
The Wrong Drawers
Something Old, Something Dead
Frame and Fortune
For Love and Cheesecake
Hoedown Showdown

~

Adventures in Ghostsitting
Desperately Seeking Salvage
Don't Dream It's Rover
Every Death You Take
Having a Ball
All Died Out

~

Other Titles
One Kiss
Liv and Breathe

Chapter One

The clink and clatter of silverware in the busy diner did nothing to block out the thoughts churning through Olivia Jameson's head. She had made the call earlier this morning, and now she would have to live with the consequences. Hoping she'd survive the experience, she had her doubts it would be easy.

"What can I get you, hon?" Betty, the owner of Petri's Dish, asked with pad and pencil in hand.

"Just coffee." At the thought of the storm she may have created, Liv's shoulders drooped.

Betty's eyes narrowed behind her thick glasses. "Tell me what's wrong. You never just order coffee, especially when I have my pineapple salsa pancakes on the Specials board." Her hand went to her hip, while her expression became mutinous. "So you're not still worrying about that little ruckus over at the Beckham farm, are you? I told you it would all blow over."

Unfortunately, it wasn't blowing over. In fact, it had just gotten a whole lot bigger. "They're pressing charges." It was as simple and as complicated as that.

"What?" Bustling around the counter, Betty plopped down on the stool next to Liv. A crowd began to gather the second she did. She never sat down for anything, not even when she wasn't working. "You better tell me what in the world is going on, right now."

No matter what she said or did at this point, Liv

knew the entire story was going to come out soon enough. Such was life in a community their size. Sometimes she wished she lived in Kissinger, the next town over, where everyone seemed to mind their own business.

She might as well take a chance and tell her side before Mr. High and Mighty came rolling into town—if he could unglue himself from his society life long enough to take any interest.

"Some boys in town say they saw my boys over in Beckham's pastures trying to tip over cows. When these town kids came along, they said they spooked the camp boys, who took off running. According to the accusers, that's how the fence was broken and how the alpacas got out and ran away. Beckham still hasn't found two of them."

By this time, there was a solid crowd of about twenty people hemming Liv and Betty in at the counter. As much as Liv appreciated the looks of outrage for her camp boys, and for the situation in general, she didn't blame the Beckhams for pressing charges. Especially with the graffiti Mr. Beckham had told her was spray-painted on the side of his barn.

She just couldn't wrap her head around the idea that her boys would do something so destructive when they knew the consequences and the punishment for not toeing the line.

"I don't believe it," Betty declared, and had the majority of the other people agreeing with her both verbally and by nodding their heads. "There's no way the boys at Breathe would jeopardize their time here by doing something so stupid."

Liv would have said the same thing to her boss,

Alex Campbell, this morning if he'd picked up his phone. Instead she'd left him a message asking him to please come to the farm, and she'd explain when he got here. It would be far better to handle this face to face. That way she could plead the case for her boys and make him understand more easily than she could convey over email. She didn't want him here, but she wasn't able to figure out a way to avoid it.

"I agree," Liv said to the diner at large, but worry still pulled her eyebrows together. "The problem is how do I prove it? I don't want to accuse anyone else, and I can't prove without a shadow of a doubt that the boys were all in their beds last night. Not even David. This is a huge mess, just in time for the annual cook-off."

"Don't you worry about the cook-off," Tim from the mechanic's shop said. "That's all taken care of, except for a few details. We'll figure something out with the boys, too. I'm coming there today to work on that car with them. I'll ask some questions that maybe you can't ask."

There was a chorus of agreement while people all went their separate ways. She really appreciated the support, but who was going to be there when Mr. Campbell came riding in to shut down the camp because she wasn't doing a good job as the director? She couldn't—and wouldn't—lose Breathe, a camp that had been around for almost eighty years. It housed underprivileged boys from major cities over the summer, giving them a chance to see real grass and real cows, to ride horses and learn skills and self-worth that would hopefully keep them out of gangs and make them productive members of society.

Life without Breathe would be pointless, since she

had no idea what else she would do. She had her son, David, and loved being his mother, but Breathe was her calling. This farm had been her dream for years, ever since her uncle had rescued her and her sisters and made them a home here. She'd even shared that dream and the beginnings of the life she'd always wanted with her late husband before he died. For eight years she'd been living it on her own and doing a good job. But now it was all at risk.

She might have to start thinking about a different future if she couldn't convince one man that this was not the excuse he'd been looking for to close the place down from the moment he'd inherited it and then completely distanced himself from the farm except to write the checks.

****

Alex Campbell's morning so far had been filled with frustrating, irritating phone calls and general chaos all the way around. As he sped north from Washington, DC to backwoods Central Pennsylvania, he gripped the wheel tightly and hoped to be in and out of there in record time. What had begun as a day with few commitments had now become one huge rash of ridiculousness.

And to top it all off, he'd lied to his mother. He would probably hear about that for the next twenty years when she found out why he had cancelled her plans to go to the opera. The opera where he was supposed to meet the lovely and eminently suitable Phoebe Lehman, who his mother thought would be perfect for him to finally settle down with.

Instead, he was on back roads with potholes that had yet to be fixed, driving his low-slung convertible and hoping against hope that no cow would be standing out in the middle of the road where he couldn't avoid it.

Because it was only a three-hour drive, he had brought an overnight bag with him in case it wasn't an open-and-shut issue. He was not planning on staying at the camp his father had loved more than anything, not for longer than a night at most. Alex would go, do his duty, whatever that was, then come home the next day. Liv had not told him why she needed him at the farm, only that she did. And then she hadn't answered her phone when he'd called for more details before derailing his whole day.

Over the years, he'd considered shutting the place down, but something always held him back. It didn't hurt his business to be able to say he helped underprivileged kids on a continuous basis. And as much as he might hate the camp because of all it had stood for in his youth, it was a write-off.

Though hate was too strong a word. He didn't give it much thought other than at tax time. When his father died, he'd left Liv as director. Until this morning, she had handled anything that came up, using her best judgment. Beyond writing checks and doing taxes, he didn't have anything to do with the camp itself. That had worked for him just fine.

But now he had been summoned—he didn't know another word for it—and so he was on his way to cow-patty heaven and avoiding his mother. Not quite what he had wanted this morning when he'd woken up in his own king-sized bed with its expensive sheets.

After twenty minutes, when he was sure he'd seen the same lightning-struck tree three times, he finally admitted defeat and stopped at a convenience store. His directions must be wrong, and his GPS had decided to quit working about five minutes ago. Hell of a time to have the thing give up on him.

Add to that the fact that he didn't know the area well enough, since he had never actually driven out here because he'd left when he was thirteen, and he was stuck with no idea where he was going or how to get there. Calling his mom was out of the question. She would give him a hard time for being out here at all. Calling Liv was also not going to happen, as he didn't want to be at a disadvantage before he even got to the camp.

A bell dinged over his head as he entered Bob's Grab and Go.

The man he assumed was Bob gave him the eye as he threaded his way through rack after rack of miscellanea.

"I was wondering if you could help me get back on the right track," Alex said, just wanting to be done with this whole journey and yet flailing around out in the middle of nowhere. He hadn't been in this area for eighteen years. In fact, he'd made a point to avoid it whenever possible, except for the funeral five years ago that had saddled him with his father's camp in the first place.

"Where ya goin', city slicker?"

Alex would have laughed if it weren't so ridiculous. If he threw his father's name around right now, he'd bet he would be treated in a totally different way. Yet he didn't want to reminisce with Bob about the old days, he just wanted to get to the right farm.

"Right outside Dillsburg, to the north."

"Well, you're almost there, dependin' on where

you're comin' from." The guy scratched his chin and stared, obviously looking for an answer to his unspoken question.

"I'm coming from Washington, DC. If you could just tell me where to go from here?"

"You made a wrong turn back at the stop sign on 114."

"And where was that?" He'd depended so heavily on his GPS that he'd just made the designated turns until Sheila, with her Australian accent, had died out on him.

"Back a ways."

"So where exactly did I go wrong back at the stop sign?" Alex asked, his frustration mounting. For some reason he could not get this guy in his overalls and trucker cap to give him a precise answer.

"Well, now, if you wanted to go on into the little burg, then you coulda turned left at the sign, or gone right, to the capital. But since you went straight across, you ended up here." The man used his thick fingers to trace the line of a red road on the map Alex had printed as a backup, just in case.

About at the end of his rope, Alex folded the computer-generated map and massaged his forehead. He squinted at the guy behind the small country store counter.

Intelligent eyes twinkled at him from under the trucker's cap that read Hal. And the slow wink did nothing to dispel Alex's tension. He didn't want to be here anyway, and now he was getting attitude from this backwoods guy. Gritting his teeth, he made a real effort not to say anything that would make it through the town's grapevine within two point three seconds.

"Should've gone to the left," the older man said out of the blue, lifting his cap and swiping his sparse hair backward.

Finally! Alex snapped the pages off the counter and made a point of saying thank you in his best office voice. He wasn't here to antagonize the locals but simply to assess the situation, use his expertise in business handling to get the full story of the incident at the farm, and then get back to his comfortable condo in DC. There was no time for detours. He should have been there almost thirty minutes ago. Glancing at his watch, he grimaced. Almost forty minutes ago.

"Got somewhere to be?" the rotund man asked, wiping his fingers on the bib of his overalls.

"Yes, I'm going to a farm to address an issue involving camp kids." It had to be them. He couldn't think of a single other reason Liv couldn't handle whatever this was on her own. At the last second, he realized he'd just invited the very conversation he hadn't wanted to have. All he needed to do was get back in his car, head toward the stop sign, and then turn left.

"Would that be Crockett's farm? The one run by Liv? That girl has a good head on her shoulders." His tone implied he couldn't believe Alex knew someone who had it so together.

Before he said anything he shouldn't, Alex forced himself to calm. He wasn't going to get into it with this man and his country store that had everything from live bait to a mini video store with DVD titles from the early nineties. "Yes, and I'm due there about an hour ago, so I'll be going." He nodded at Hal. "Thanks for the directions. I go back to the stop sign and turn left then, is it?"

"Not unless you want to go back the way you came, you won't." He scratched his chin again.

Alex suppressed a sigh. He did want to go back the way he came, but he'd made a promise. And he kept his promises, no matter how ridiculous they seemed after he had time to really think about what he'd committed himself to. "So do I go right, then?"

"Now you got the idea. Shouldn't be too far down the road, especially in that fancy car you got."

Alex made sure to thank Hal again before exiting the store and inhaling the fresh outside air. He preferred the exhaust and fumes of DC where he worked, but reminded himself that he wouldn't be here for long. He could handle the great outdoors for a short time.

And it would be fine to see the old homestead again. It had been a while since he'd been out this way. It wasn't going to kill him to relax and enjoy the scenery a little. Besides, if he remembered correctly, time was but a small thought out here. You got there when you got there. So he'd drive slow, take in the scenery, and maybe avoid seeing the farm for a little while longer. His manager wouldn't mind in the least.

****

"Where the heck is he?" Bill Jameson paced the spacious kitchen and turned at the oversized refrigerator. He came back with his hands in his gray hair and his shirt bunched at his belt buckle.

Since her uncle was only repeating what she'd asked four times already, Liv tipped her glass of lemonade to her lips, wishing the man wasn't coming at all. Fortunately David was out playing with all the other boys, so she and Bill could talk candidly without his little eight-year-old ears around. "I'm sure he'll get here when he gets here. He probably got lost without all his one-way streets and tons of street signs."

Bill gave her the disapproving scowl she'd gotten when she was fifteen and snuck out to see her boyfriend. "You're not going to antagonize him every moment he's here, are you?"

"Who, me?" she asked innocently.

"Yes, you. Please, Liv, I want this visit to go as smoothly as possible."

"I could have handled this on my own if Beckham would have listened to me. But he wouldn't, so I'm stuck. But I wish I hadn't called *him*. *He's* going to act like visiting royalty, and you know it," she grumbled.

"We do need him here. This is his farm, after all, and he has to handle something this big. Plus, I'm sure he could use the rest and relaxation."

"Rest and relaxation?" she asked incredulously. "With twenty kids here and a possible lawsuit on our hands? What planet are you living on?"

"That's the attitude I'm talking about." Her uncle wrung his hands, sidling onto a stool at the island in the middle of the kitchen. "I'm not going to be able to do this if you and he are at each other's throats."

"Please. I wouldn't ever dare do that to him. My job is too important to me. And this is David's home. Besides, Alex barely acknowledges me when I email him, and I've been left to manage this place by myself for years. The last time he was here was when he was twenty-five. Even then he wouldn't come to the farm, just went right from the funeral home in town to the lawyer's office before heading back to DC. It's not going to be any different this time. Once the problem is fixed, he'll leave again and hopefully never come back."

Her uncle groaned. For just a minute, Liv considered apologizing, along with promising she wouldn't cause any waves, or let the ones Alex made do anything except drift over her.

But Bill went on. "You have a habit of sticking your foot in it. I want to make sure that's not going to pop up here anywhere. I want you to be nice to him and help out if he needs anything."

"Not in my job description." She tipped the glass to her lips again and swallowed the tart lemonade while she swallowed the rest of the words that wanted to come spilling out of her mouth. Alex was no real prize to get along with, even over the phone, which she'd had the misfortune of using on several occasions when he called to clarify what an email couldn't get across. But she wasn't going to make this more difficult for the man she loved and trusted. And she wasn't going to lose the only home her son had ever known. "I'm sure we won't have much to say to each other, and when we do talk, I'll be absolutely certain to be nice and sweet."

When Bill's eyes lit with hope, Liv reined in the thoughts tumbling through her mind. Just because she thought Alex was a jerk didn't mean everyone else thought so too. Long ago, he must have had some redeeming qualities after growing up early on with her heroes, Bill and Crockett, before his mom whisked him away to refinement and the city. That was the summer she'd been brought here, and he'd left within two weeks.

"I'd really appreciate it if you'd tone it down over the next couple of days."

Liv struggled with not being offended. "I do not need to tone anything down, Uncle Bill. He'll arrive at some point, he'll fix things, and then he'll leave." Leaning back against the counter in the big country kitchen, she cradled her sweating glass. "Don't pin any hopes on him staying. I don't want to see you hurt."

Bill ran an agitated hand through his short hair, pulling it at the roots. "I know, Liv, and I also know this isn't going to be easy for any of us. But you need him to figure out what we can do as far as those boys who are in trouble. We can't send them home with records."

Liv held up a hand, stalling the next part of the lecture she'd heard five times over the last three hours since she'd been texted that Alex the Great condescended to join them on the humble farm in Central Pennsylvania. She'd missed his call, and his voice message had been short, basically along the lines of *What do you want?* Before she'd had a chance to call him back, a text had come: *Three hours. Be ready to explain yourself.* Just that, nothing else. "You think I don't know that? We're supposed to be a safe place, and now I might have to explain juvenile charges to their parents. I'm doing everything I can." She narrowed her eyes at him. "But I'm also thinking you have an ulterior motive, or you wouldn't be so worried about his visit. We already run pretty efficiently here."

Bill didn't take the bait she'd so obviously thrown out there. "All I ask is that you be nice to him when he's here, no matter how much of a pain he can be."

And that was no lie. The last time Alex had been in this area, he'd barely nodded at Liv. He had no idea about her life or those who were important to her. She'd never even told him she'd gotten married or that she had a son. It was none of his business. As long as she kept the farm running and in the black, he had no reason to involve himself. Unfortunately, that had all changed with the damage done next door.

Now she'd have to rely on him to get the charges dropped. Something Mr. Beckham refused to even speak with her about.

"Please, Liv?" Bill even clasped his hands in front of his broad chest and gave her the pleading eyes.

She laughed, she couldn't help it. Smacking him in the arm, she put down her glass and stepped in for a quick hug. "You can count on me. I just hope we can count on him. But there better be a raise in it for me at the end." She was gratified when he laughed with her. She owed this man her life and tried to show him every day how much that meant to her.

"You really are the best, Liv. No matter what anyone else tells you." She groaned when he laughed again. "In all honesty, I don't know what we'd do without you. Promise me you won't go anywhere, while you're making promises."

She wasn't her sisters. Nothing could drag her away. "I love it here. I love the kids who come in and spend the summer with us from Philly and Harrisburg. I wouldn't leave for anything in the world. I love that David is growing up on a farm and seeing all sides of life." This was their home, and she was lucky to have it. She couldn't imagine being anywhere else, or wanting to be anywhere else.

A horse neighed out in the pasture, followed by a cow lowing. Glancing out the window, she saw a car tearing up the long gravel drive from the main road.

Looked like his highness was finally here.

Bill grabbed her hand, keeping her immobile in the kitchen while they listened to the squeal of brakes on the macadam parking lot behind the house. A door slammed. It had been more like four hours instead of three, but her reprieve was over.

Show time.

Chapter Two

Arriving at the farm was like stepping back in time. Alex had played on the tire swing in the big oak tree as soon as he was old enough to run. The sweet smell of cut grass reminded him of fresh laundry hung from the line out back and kids screaming through the lowering dusk with flashlights and tag on their minds.

He shook all that off to find his dad's old friend Bill barreling through the front door like the prodigal son had returned. The beefy man's arms were open and his smile huge.

Alex didn't know whether to run or duck. Both options were taken out of his hands when Bill nearly tackled him and crushed him, almost bringing him to his knees.

"It's so good to see you here, boy." Bill hugged tighter, and Alex didn't know if he could survive any more pressure. Just when he thought he might burst, Bill let go to hold him at arm's length. "I can't believe how much you look like him."

"Yes, well." Alex stepped back from the bigger man's grasp, straightening his tie and smoothing his button-down shirt. "It's good to see you, Bill. I hadn't realized you still worked here."

"Of course he does."

That voice was one he rarely heard, preferring to do business by email or through the regular post when he had to be involved at all. But it had taken him from his normal Monday morning routine and had thrust him out to this memory-filled country scene. It was going to take some serious work to separate past from present in this place, but hopefully he wouldn't be here long enough to do more than skim through that small chapter of long ago.

"Liv," he said, turning toward her with a vague memory of a skinny girl in boys' shorts and a tank top. What he got was an eyeful of something much more grown up—and furious, from his calculations.

"Alex." She crossed her arms over her chest and tried to stare him down from her height of nearly five and a half feet tall. He'd stared down trustees that were twice her size. He wouldn't have any problem putting her in her place.

"So, you called, I came. I am prepared to handle the damage if you just tell me who to talk to."

She eyed him from head to toe like he was something distasteful on her shoe. "Let's do this in my office. No need to stand out here. Bill, if you could bring some lemonade, I'd appreciate it."

****

The office still looked exactly as it had when his father was here. Liv wondered if he remembered that or if it was so long ago he'd forgotten. She hadn't moved a thing after Crockett died and left her as the manager.

She wavered for a second about letting Alex have the chair behind the desk because, technically, he was the owner. But then she walked faster to get there before he could. She was in charge of this operation and wanted him to see that from the get-go.

"Have a seat," she said, indicating one of the two

leather club chairs from a bygone era. Alex lifted a dark eyebrow before choosing the chair on the left while she sat down behind the enormous oak desk. Arranging a few papers to her satisfaction, Liv took a moment to compose herself.

"I'm not planning on being here very long. If you could just get to the point of your very urgent message that you felt you couldn't expound on in my voicemail, then I can get whatever it is cleared up and go back to my job and my home." He set his briefcase down at his feet, crossed one ankle over the other knee, and folded his hands over his stomach.

His attitude was bad enough, but his posture and his demeanor irritated her further. Who did he think he was? He couldn't spend a few days with these kids that had meant so much to his father? Couldn't get his hands dirty just once, helping someone less fortunate than himself with anything more than his checkbook?

Before she said anything foolish, she pulled herself back. She didn't want him here anyway, and liked running the camp without his interference. Not wanting to change that made her keep her lips sealed for a few extra seconds and gave him time to get himself going again.

"If I remember correctly, and I do, you called me here to do something. I dropped everything to come, and now you're just staring at me. So I'll ask again, what am I doing here?"

It felt like glass in her mouth, but she forced herself to say, "We have a problem, and I need your help."

Her uncle delivered the lemonade at that point, giving her a chance to swallow the tart drink and get herself back in check.

****

Normally Alex liked helping people. He helped businesses that were going under to restructure their plan, to accommodate their resources, and stay open. He'd helped his friend paint her condo one day. You wanted someone to check your goldfish or water your plants while you were on vacation? He had no problem with that. But this—this he wasn't sure he wanted to do.

There was a part of him that felt selfish for not being more willing, but he ruthlessly shoved that part away and sat there, waiting for her to continue. She was the one who had called him.

Her huffed-out breath did interesting things to the T-shirt she wore with the camp logo right below her left collarbone. He didn't remember authorizing company shirts, but he had to admit that it looked good on her.

"Fine." She picked up a pencil and twirled it between her long fingers with their unpolished nails. "We had an incident at the Beckham farm down the road. They're threatening to press charges on some of the boys here, saying that they vandalized their barn, broke a fence, and made them lose two animals."

Sitting back in his chair, he tried to absorb what she'd just said. This was worse than he'd thought. The last thing he needed was a crisis, especially one where he had to be involved. And he'd have to be involved in this one.

Legally, Liv could handle nearly anything, but this was not one of those things. For a brief second Alex wished his father were still here to take over. It did no good to wish for it to be different, though. He'd just have to take this in hand. Surely the Beckhams would understand reason once he spoke with them. They

18

would drop the charges, and then he could go back to Washington, DC.

"I'll go speak to them. I'm sure Mr. Beckham will be open to discussing this like rational adults. We can pay for any damages and move forward."

His announcement, one he thought was a good solution, obviously did not sit well with Liv. Her fists clenched on the desktop where his father had played cars with him.

"What?" he said, sitting up straight in the leather chair.

"Aren't you going to even consider that the boys here didn't do this?"

"No, I'm not." He rose from his chair, the same one where he'd sat when his dad would hold him in his lap in the last few seconds of the day before bedtime, when he was little, and grabbed his briefcase from the floor. "I'll be back after I talk to Mr. Beckham. I'm sure we can get this handled quickly."

Striding out of the room, he already had his best approach running through his mind and his plan of attack if Plan A didn't work. This was his area of expertise. He could placate the man next door, who had been there forever. He remembered Mr. Harold Beckham as fair and jovial. Even though it had been several years since he had talked to the man, someone's true nature never changed.

****

Pulling up to the old farmhouse out in the middle of the field, Alex put his car into park. He took a moment to stare at the fresh paint and the weed-free front garden while he reviewed what he was going to say and how he was going to say it. He wouldn't be dealing with some guy with a master's degree in finance and twenty years in the rat race behind him. So his approach needed to be better suited to a farmer who had worked and lived on the land for the last sixty years, pulling a living from stubborn soil.

After straightening his tie, he briefly wished he had taken the time to change into jeans and a polo shirt. If he was going for wishes, he actually wished Liv had not called him in the first place. But here he was. He hadn't had to do much in the years since his father had died. Without a doubt, he could take on this hiccup.

His knock went unanswered. He stood for another few seconds waiting to see if it was simply taking Mr. Beckham a while to get to the front door. But then he heard yelling from the back of the house. Most likely whoever was going on and on back there would know where the owner was and how to find him.

When Alex tromped around back, he found a scene of absolute chaos. A mass of hay looked like it had exploded on the ground around the front of the barn. Several men in T-shirts, jeans, and boots wrangled a cow away from the mess toward the open pasture to the left. He knew enough to step back and stay back until they finished their chore or he was liable to get trampled.

A dog barked anxiously, circling the legs of an older man, but not one Alex thought was old enough to be Mr. Beckham. The man shouted, and for the second time in a day Alex was transported back to the time before he was thirteen. He remembered that very voice bellowing out in the field while Alex played in the pond on the back of their acreage, or laughing at some bawdy joke his dad had told over whiskey in the big country kitchen after the camp boys had gone home for the summer and the real work started.

He shook himself out of his momentary trek back in time. He would just approach the old guy and reason with him. There was history here, even if it wasn't Alex's history anymore. No way would the man press charges against Alex's father's pet project. It just wouldn't happen.

Still, he hung back until the coast was a little clearer. He watched as two guys grabbed the rope they had thrown around the cow's neck and tried to wrestle the animal to the gate into the pasture. He didn't know what the two guys weighed, nor did he remember how heavy a cow was, but it looked like a losing battle for the humans.

Finally, the old man stepped in and swatted the cow on the rump, which got it moving, trailing the two guys with their hands on the rope behind it. There was a lot of cursing and yelling, but the cow led the way while Mr. Beckham turned and zeroed in on Alex.

He definitely should have taken the time to put some jeans on, especially when confronted with Mr. Beckham's disapproving head-to-toe look. The man pulled at the collar of his plaid shirt, reached down to pat his faithful dog, and strolled over as if he had all the time in the world. And maybe he did.

"What can I do for you, son?" His voice was no less booming up close, as if he no longer had a volume control.

"I'm here about some trouble you've had," Alex yelled, figuring the guy was hard of hearing.

He figured wrong.

"There's no need to yell when you're standing ten

feet away. I bet Bossy heard you over in the pasture, with that bit of gruff. I'm old, not deaf, boy." His fingers hooked into his pockets as he rocked back on his heels. If Alex had been asked what the quintessential farmer looked like, this would be it. His grandfather had dressed the same way before he'd died. His father had resisted the temptation as long as Alex had lived here, and he'd always dressed in slacks when he'd come to Baltimore to visit him three times a year. But that didn't mean he hadn't dressed differently at his home.

Alex hadn't owned a flannel shirt since he was thirteen. His mother had donated them all as soon as they'd driven out of town. Clearing his throat, Alex also cleared the memory from his mind.

"Mr. Beckham, do you happen to have a moment? There's something I want to talk with you about, if you can make the time."

"Now that Bossy is taken care of, I'm sure the boys can handle the rest without me breathing down their necks. Come in, and we'll see if Mrs. Beckham can whip us up some sweet tea." He started off in his stiff gait, the dog trailing at his heels. After two steps, he turned around. "Why haven't we seen you around all these years, sonny? I know your ma kept you away when he was alive, but the least you could have done was come back after he was dead."

Alex didn't owe anyone an explanation, but dealings would go much more smoothly if he said something here. "I've kept the place open. I've been the silent owner all these years, keeping his dream alive."

All he got for his avoidance was a raised eyebrow.

When Mr. Beckham turned again without another

word, Alex followed the old man into the house, against his better judgment. He had a feeling he had just lost the upper hand. He wasn't sure if he was going to be able to get it back.

****

"Oh, I could seriously clobber that blockhead." Liv stomped through the kitchen with murder on her mind.

"Can't kill the boss," her uncle said. "Here, why don't you tenderize this chicken? It'll give you something constructive to do."

She didn't want to pulverize chicken. She wanted Alex to see that those boys would never have vandalized another property, and that they deserved to be believed. They deserved to have him know they hadn't done the spray painting on the side of Mr. Beckham's barn. They would never have done that. But instead of listening to her, he had galloped off with his checkbook.

"Is it really too much to ask that Alex see that these kids aren't bad? That they would never have put us, or themselves, in this position?"

"He hasn't been here in years, hon. Maybe he's forgotten what it takes for these kids to get here at all." Bill rolled a piece of chicken in crushed corn flakes. Just the thought of her uncle's secret-recipe fried chicken set her stomach to grumbling.

"The faster you pound, the faster lunch's on the table. It might make you feel better, too."

"I highly doubt it." But she took the mallet anyway and began pounding that chicken breast like it had kicked her dog. And she did feel marginally better. Talking with her uncle helped even more.

"I just don't get why he won't even consider that

the boys were not the culprits. It could have been anyone. Just because Jake Foster said it was my boys doesn't mean that vindictive teen is right."

"I told you not to mess with him, and you didn't believe me. He might be young, but he has a lot of muscle and money behind him. No one is going to doubt him for a second."

"Yeah, well, I doubt him, and so should Alex. I can't believe that man went over to Mr. Beckham's with his checkbook in hand. I don't want the boys to be thought of as guilty in all this. This will not look good on our record, and it certainly won't do anything for their sense of self-worth."

Bill handed her another piece of chicken, slipping the one she had almost pulverized into nothing out from under her vengeful mallet.

"I think that one's done." He laughed and she joined him, leaning against his shoulder to hold herself up.

She willed the tears away even as she smiled. They would fix this, and it would be done right. As much as she wanted the charges dropped, she hoped Alex was failing miserably at getting Mr. Beckham to sweep it under the carpet with a little cash outlay. Yes, it would keep the kids from having a permanent record, but it would also be a huge black mark that would be difficult, if not impossible, to wipe away.

And then he might have the ammunition she worried would give him the right to shut this place down. She wasn't sure why he hadn't, but maybe if she figured out a way to convince him of the good they were doing, she'd never have to worry about it again.

She didn't want him here, but if he had to be

because his checkbook didn't work, then she would use her time wisely.

****

The sweet tea in Alex's glass was forming cavities in his mouth just by him looking at it. He could probably stand a spoon up in the stuff, but somehow he was going to have to figure out a way to choke down at least a few sips. Mrs. Beckham was watching.

"So what did you want?"

Alex didn't remember the man being this belligerent. Perhaps it was something new in the last few years. Or maybe it was because of the situation. Alex was combating more than he'd thought, if the latter was the case. The Mr. Beckham of his youth was the kind of guy who would have thrown the ball back to you even if you'd just shattered his window with your wild pitch.

Alex and his friends had broken one of his fences horsing around when they were ten, and, while the old man had asked them to fix it, he'd also helped them by showing them the right way to do it and then providing them with lunch and drinks. When they were done, he'd also given them each ten dollars for their work.

This man looked as if he'd like to spit in Alex's eye.

After clearing his throat, Alex gave his most encouraging smile and amped up the charm when he looked at Mrs. Beckham. "I'm here because I was called by my director regarding an issue with some vandalism on your property, sir."

"What about it? I've already spoken to the police." Beckham harrumphed and squinted at Alex.

"I understood that you had and were planning on

pressing charges. I was hoping to come to an agreement with you outside the police and have you drop the charges. I can guarantee that these boys will not harm your property again, and I'm willing to pay to fix the damage." Leaning forward, he retrieved his checkbook and pen from his breast pocket. He'd thought about how much it might cost him. While it wouldn't drain him in any way, it might take a bite out of the budget for the camp. Liv would just have to come up with a way to deal with the fallout. His job was to get the mess contained. She would be the real cleaner.

"And just how much money do you think you're going to have to throw at this thing to make it go away?"

Alex's hand paused in the act of dating the check as he looked up at the old guy. Normally he was a whiz at reading people and their price tag, but he couldn't see anything on Mr. Beckham's face except a frown.

After naming a figure that he thought was more than generous, Alex continued to write the check.

"Hogwash!"

Mrs. Beckham folded her hands over her breast and gasped. "Harry!"

"No, Darcy, this isn't going to wash away with dollars." His gaze narrowed back in on Alex. "Why do you think that's enough? Do you even know what the real damage was? Or are you just pulling a number out of your rear end to try and make me fall in with whatever you want?"

His mind running at a hundred thoughts a second, Alex tried to salvage the conversation. "The director told me there was damage to several of your outbuildings with spray paint and vulgarities carved into some of the wood. A fence was broken and several animals have yet to be found. In keeping with the rate of new paint and possibly replacing several boards on the structures, I felt this was approximately the necessary money to do that, along with a sizeable amount for your pain and suffering." Alex put his pen down on the coffee table in front of him and abandoned the check. This was not the easy meeting he had hoped for. Not even the slightly uneasy one he had resigned himself to when he'd followed the man into the house.

"My pain and suffering. Bah!" The dog at his feet howled. "I don't want or need your money. I want someone's blood and sweat over here. I want someone to be responsible for just once, by God. And I'm going to get it if I have to press those charges all the way to having those responsible arrested and carted away to the pokey."

Alex sat back in his chair, blown away. Obviously, he had not seen this side of Beckham before. It made him wonder briefly what else he didn't know between childhood and now. He got back to business before he could say something that would betray his confusion.

"I'm sorry we couldn't come to an agreement, sir. I'll let you get back to your tea. Have a wonderful afternoon, ma'am."

If he'd had a hat he would have tipped it. As it was, he simply made his way out of the house with a sure stride and the determination to find out what he could do to change this man's mind. He had a place to start, though. He'd round up the kids who'd done this, and he'd have them apologize and get to work with their hands, backs, and sweat to fix this mess.

Chapter Three

Pacing the living room was not helping Liv. Not that she had thought it would, but she hadn't been able to come up with any better ideas.

Oh, how she wished there was some simple way to prove the boys hadn't been out at the Beckham farm that night, and therefore get them off the hook. She had her suspicions as to who was actually responsible, but no way to make them confess. Her frustration level was about to hit the red line if Alex didn't come back soon.

She'd sent all the boys out to play with some water guns and a bucket full of water balloons. It was topping ninety outside, easily. Not only would the water cool them off, but it would give her some peace and quiet to think. She couldn't do that with them hanging around or squabbling as they had been prone to do lately, with the tensions rising.

Several of the older boys had been caught threatening the other boys to find out who had done this. They'd had to be brought into her office and talked to about standing together and innocent until proven guilty. She didn't know if she had really reached them, since two of the four were newbies this year. The other two had been sullen even as they said they understood. The upside was that no one had made any more noise about it the rest of the day. The car restoration from this morning was well on its way, and the tie-dyeing for field day had gone smoothly.

So now they were outside getting the energy out, and she was in here feeling trapped while waiting for an all-grown-up Alex to make an appearance.

And he sure had grown up well. She had an image of him in her mind that came mainly from a picture his dad had kept on his desk. A small boy with a cowlick in his light brown hair and laughing blue eyes. The hair was darker now and the eyes no longer laughing, but he was still able to make her heart flutter.

When she'd first arrived at Breathe, with Bill, she'd been so scared she hadn't registered anyone or anything except that she and her little sisters were finally safe and her uncle was keeping them. After the first week, she'd noticed Alex and had thought he was cute, in her eleven-year-old mind, but then he was gone, and the court battles had started.

She'd heard tidbits here and there about Alex's mother and the fight she was willing to wage to keep Alex away from the farm. She'd done just that, making him far removed from what the camp stood for and from his dad. What would have happened if he'd stayed?

She didn't know and wasn't willing to go down that line of thought at the moment.

The plus side, though, was that this attraction was at least one thing she could control. She'd ruthlessly shove it away, and they could go back to email correspondence and the occasional phone call. She'd ignore the way she had a face to go with that gravelly voice now, one that wasn't from a company brochure or the website for Breathe.

And then the man himself was standing in the

doorway of the living room, looking a little worse for wear with his shirt untucked and a splash of something plastering the fabric to his impressive chest.

She tried to look away, she really did, but there was something mesmerizing about seeing the faint shadow of chest hair through the transparent shirt, with a hint of the ridges of muscle underneath.

"I'm up here," he said, making her gaze snap back to his.

Heat flared in her cheeks.

"How did it go?" she asked, completely sidestepping his loaded comment.

"Not too much better than my walk from the car to the house. In fact, better than my walk here, since Mr. Beckham didn't think to physically throw anything at me."

He stepped fully into the room, then headed past her to the kitchen. His whole backside was wet. And while this sight was also intriguing, it made her want to laugh. She kept the snicker in with monumental effort and was glad she did when he turned around a split second later.

"I need to talk to you, but first I obviously have to change. When is dinner, and is there a place we can eat without extra ears hanging on our every word?"

There was only one place she could think of where they would be guaranteed privacy, but she didn't know if she was willing to spend even an hour in her cottage with his presence taking up all the space and changing the very air inside her sanctuary.

****

So did you take a gift of some sort to your camp director's cottage for dinner? Alex mulled over the question for about two seconds before he realized this was a business dinner. As such, he didn't need to bring anything but himself. And it was a little early for wine. Not to mention he was positive Liv would frown at him for having alcohol around her precious boys.

He finished combing his hair, ignoring how naked he felt without a tie. After his shower he had decided to go with those jeans and polo shirt that he should have worn earlier to talk to Harry Beckham. He still wasn't entirely positive how it had all gone to shit so quickly, but that was one of the reasons he wanted to talk with Liv this evening. They needed a different Plan B, since the one he'd originally thought of was not going to fly. If Harry wanted blood and sweat from the people who did the mischief, he wouldn't settle for a new barn out of Alex's personal checking account.

So he was out of ideas and figured it was time to ask the woman who was actually a part of this community and knew how things worked. Hopefully she would be reasonable. He had a few ideas that he needed her input on, but if she shut him out during the conversation, as she had before, then they were going to get nowhere fast.

He did end up deciding to pick a couple of flowers on his way from the house to the cottage out back, just to lessen the tension.

How little he knew.

"You didn't pick those from your mother's old gardens, did you? The boys work on those every day to keep the weeds out and keep them looking beautiful. You destroyed the symmetry with a careless swipe of your hand." She glared at him.

He kept coming forward through the front door,

forcing her to back up or meet him chest to chest. He knew which he would have preferred, no matter how stupid it was.

"I picked exactly one flower from each of the sections, and they don't look the worse for wear. My father planted those to be enjoyed, not just looked at and kept pristine. What's the use of flowers if you can't touch them and enjoy them fully with as many senses as possible?"

He'd finally managed to shut her up. It should have felt better, but his own words had thrown him back to the summer his father had planted all those flowers for his mother. Crockett had said those very words when Alex's mother had complained about him bringing her a clutch of them, the summer before they'd left for good.

He shook the memory off. It wouldn't help with the discussion they needed to have.

"Look, we have a lot to talk about and not much time before dinner breaks up. I understand you'll need to get back to your kid-watching duties as soon as that happens."

Her lips were still pursed, but she betrayed herself by stroking the petals of one of the irises in her hands. "So talk."

"I'm hungry. Can we at least sit down and eat something? Whatever Bill sent over smells delicious."

"Bill sent over the same thing the boys are having. Homemade fried chicken and mashed potatoes." She turned away from him, with the flowers still clutched in her hand, before he could read her expression.

Following along behind her, he honestly couldn't remember the last time he'd eaten full-on homemade anything. The closest he got was opening a package from the freezer and throwing it into a pan. Even his mother was more apt to order out than cook in her pristine, top-of-the-line kitchen. She always said she had spent too many years in the country. Now that she lived in the city she wanted to take advantage of the amenities at her fingertips, like Chinese, Thai, or Italian food at the touch of her speed dial.

Though he tried, he kept catching himself watching the sway of Liv's hips as she made her way across the linoleum floor of her cozy kitchen. Above the sink, bright yellow curtains hung at the window looking out over the barnyard. She'd have a perfect view of the rising sun. When he found himself wondering if she'd ever enjoyed that pleasure with someone in her homey cottage, he decided all this fresh air was driving him crazy.

Fortunately, her sharp tongue brought him crashing back to firm ground that didn't involve wishing or wanting.

"Have a seat. I'll grab the food so we get this finished, and you can go back to whatever ridiculously important things you have to do that don't involve Breathe."

"That's not fair." He pulled out a chair at the round table in the middle of the kitchen, then sat with his arms propped on the well-used wood. A scar ran the length of the table in front of him, several veins radiating from the original crack. She should replace this. He knew perfectly well how much he paid her. She could afford more than this shabby furniture.

"It might not be fair, but it's certainly true." She put the flowers in a vase. When she placed them on the table smack dab in the middle of the line, the glass whacked against the scarred wood with a loud bang.

"You have anything you want to get off your chest to clear the air before we deal with the important issues here?" he asked.

The mutinous expression on her face told him he was either about to get it but good or she was straining with all she had to keep her tirade locked behind her clenched teeth.

Her better judgment seemed to have won, because she began bringing dishes to the table and placing them more gently onto the surface. "Tell me how it went with Mr. Beckham today."

Blowing out a breath he hadn't been aware he was holding, he ran a hand through his hair. "It did not go well."

"I could have told you that. Tell me something I don't know."

"How about if I tell you I could use a break here from your attitude and smart mouth?"

"Not going to happen. Continue." She brought one more bowl to the table, this one filled with mashed potatoes, and seated herself on the other side of the flowers.

He couldn't see her face. That wasn't going to work for him if they were going to strategize.

Without asking for her permission, he stood with the vase in his hand and moved it to the counter next to the sink. He was not going to have a conversation with flora when she was sitting right across from him. But then the spark in her green eyes caught him and he wished he were hiding behind the flowers again.

"Can we start over?" He didn't know what had possessed him to ask that question, but it seemed important.

The side of her luscious mouth quirked up. "At which point do you think we should start from, Alex? Where we were kids and you used to laugh and play with me in the pond? Or when you left and your dad grieved every day? When you first deigned to call me something other than Ms. Jameson because you realized I was actually going to see this camp through? Or when you stepped out of your fancy car with your attitude on, telling me how best to approach neighbors you haven't seen or dealt with in over twenty years? Pick. I'm happy to try."

Her expression and her tone of voice said differently. He sat studying her for a moment and decided to bypass that whole conversation. He'd have to think of the import of the particular times she'd chosen to highlight another time.

"Let's just start now with figuring out what the best course of action is moving forward. Do you mind if I dig in, or did you want me to stare at the food all night as penance?"

****

Crap, she'd tipped her hand over way too far by saying far too much. And now she had no idea how to get it back. So she went with his obvious preference and blocked it, pretending she hadn't pointed out every time he had disappointed her in the past.

"It's just chicken, but there are mashed potatoes and succotash to go with it. Gravy's in the pitcher to your right."

Concentrating on serving herself, she avoided his eyes altogether. She couldn't have been stupider if she had tried. There was nothing for it, though, but to forge ahead as if the events she'd chosen to pick out weren't significant. She was a master of masking, and it didn't fail her now.

Watching Alex tuck into the food on her secondhand plates did something to her stomach. They'd called a moratorium on talking through the meal, or at least the first part of it. He ate as if he hadn't had a home-cooked meal in forever. And maybe that was true up in his high, fancy townhouse in Washington, DC, far away from the peons of the world.

She knew that wasn't a fair assessment of him, but she wasn't willing to be fair right now.

He took his last bite of succotash, using the side of his finger to make sure every piece of corn and lima bean was on the fork tines before popping it into his mouth and closing his eyes.

Her succotash was not swoon-worthy, but you couldn't tell it from the low hum in the back of his throat that set all her feminine parts humming right along with it.

She cleared her throat. "If you're done, I think we should talk about what happened at Harry's today and plan accordingly."

"What happened at Harry's today was that I bombed phenomenally. I don't think I've ever had a deal go south faster than that. He was set against me from the first, but he did give me an alternative to the charges, one I think we can live with."

That was actually more than she had hoped for. She'd been told by the police not to talk to Mr. Beckham after the incident, and the man had avoided her phone calls. Even sending her Uncle Bill over hadn't made anything positive happen. The whole farm shut down around them. The Beckhams hadn't exactly been best friends with Breathe before the incident, but it was even worse now. Things had been different when Crockett was alive, but now that he wasn't, she hadn't gained the same amount of respect and camaraderie with her neighbors as Crockett had.

"And what is this deal? Why didn't you say that when you first came home instead of making me feel like all was lost?"

His shrug infuriated her. He might not care about Breathe, but she did.

"Don't be coy now, Alex. Tell me what he said."

"You're not going to like it."

"What do you care if I like it or not? Just tell me."

"Fine." He raised his hands in the air as if surrendering. She knew it was a pose. Alex would never surrender unless he had a contingency plan. "He wants the boys who did this over there. He wants their sweat and blood to paint that barn and fix the outbuildings. It's the only thing that would make him change his mind about pressing charges."

That was not going to go over well with her campers, not to mention that she was speechless with anger herself.

Chapter Four

Liv was afraid she was going to wear a hole in the linoleum with all the pacing she'd been doing over the last hour since Alex left. She'd done her duties with the boys without saying a word about the dilemma, then retreated to her cottage while they played games in the rec room. David stayed, too, as he usually did when there were kids at the camp. He liked to be in the thick of things, and she let him, believing it was best for an eight-year-old boy who had a lot of energy and a huge heart.

It was still light outside on the hot August evening, but she swore she could have slept for the whole night at this point, if given the chance.

After Alex dropped his bomb, he left without dessert. She'd had Bill pull a Shoofly Pie from the freezer, remembering that it had been Alex's favorite, and now she'd have to eat the whole sticky thing herself.

Who was she kidding? She'd already eaten three quarters of it when worrying earlier, and now she felt sick to her stomach on top of her legs hurting from all the unnecessary exercise. At least she may have already walked off all those calories.

She wasn't sure what the right thing to do was, going forward. The boys would absolutely revolt if she told them they all had to go clean Mr. Beckham's barn and outbuildings, as he seemed to want in order to be appeased. She was still convinced they had not done anything. Yet they would all have to take the punishment. If only she could figure out who had really done this so she could get them out of it altogether.

But no one was going to step forward with the information she wanted, when no one had yet. Most of the town appreciated the camp and what it was doing, but there were factions out there that would have been happier if this place was some kind of vacation farm with city people pretending to rope fake cows, instead of having these inner-city boys.

With her shins burning, she finally sat down. Dropping her head into her hands, she wondered what she could do to make this better and to make the announcement go down more smoothly, that being an announcement that she was taking away several classes tomorrow, ones the boys were looking forward to, because they would all—all of them from the youngest to the staff—be painting the neighbor's barn and replacing planks on the damaged outbuildings. And possibly finding a few animals, though she didn't know precisely how they were going to do that if they hadn't been found already.

Before she could change her mind, and despite the time, she called Harry Beckham, told him they would do it, and asked if she could check things out before the sun went completely down over the horizon. The farmer kept early hours out of habit, still going to bed right after *Jeopardy* ended at eight, but he told her she could come around so she would know what kinds of supplies to bring.

It was better than being hung up on, of course, but

she was having a hard time convincing herself of that.

Cramming her feet into a pair of work boots, she grabbed her flashlight, a measuring tape, and her keys. Might as well get this done right now so she could possibly sleep and come up with some brilliant idea on how to get the boys to agree to this. Because as much as she could force them to do it, she didn't want that to be part of their experience here. They had too much forced on them in their city lives. This was supposed to be a little piece of heaven for them, a sanctuary. And now she was taking that away. No thanks to Alex.

****

Alex hadn't been able to settle down for the evening no matter how much he tried. It boiled down to several things that altogether made it impossible. The lack of noise outside. The subtle hints that a gaggle of boys were residing in the same house with him. The anger Liv had displayed when he'd only been trying to do what she asked.

His thoughts had kept him up and doing nothing productive.

When he'd tried to sit down and answer email, a swarm of giggles came from the room down the hall. He'd heard Bill tromp down the hall and quiet the boys, but he hadn't been able to get back into work after that. After surfing the web for nothing in particular, he picked up a book he'd brought along with him just in case.

Nothing distracted him from reliving the look of total disappointment on Liv's face when he'd told her the boys would have to work off the damage that she was convinced they hadn't done.

But who else would it have been? He couldn't see

one of the locals deciding to do that much vandalism for nothing. While he'd only lived here through his thirteenth birthday, and had gotten into his fair share of trouble, those in the community respected each other, for the most part. He and his friends had done stuff like cow tipping or daring each other to run into the pond with only their underwear on. But they'd never ruined anything with their high-jinks. This sleepy town wasn't much different now than it had been then. No way had the next generation been raised to think these things were acceptable.

Yet the kinds of words and the style of the spray painting on the barn was definitely something that an inner-city kid would know how to do. He'd checked it out before he left the farm.

Why couldn't Liv see that? The answer there was easy. These kids were hers, just like they had been Crockett's. They could do no wrong in her eyes, just like they hadn't done anything wrong in Crockett's eyes all those long years ago. And that was how it had been before Alex's mother had torn him away from here and made a new life for them in a more urban setting.

Speaking of his mother, he couldn't believe she hadn't called him a hundred times already. He deliberately hadn't told her where he was going. She would have had a conniption fit. Yet when he'd checked his messages on his cell phone to see if he'd missed something, there was nothing there.

Indecision and unrest sent him outside in the lowering dusk. Night didn't fully come until almost nine out here in the wide-open spaces. The boys were in their rooms for the night because they had to get up early in the morning. It didn't mean they would be asleep, though. Who at that age wanted to sleep at seven?

A glow of light rested on the horizon, gilding everything at the back of the house with a sheen of late sunlight. The silhouettes of the buildings blended with the trees that surrounded the house, making it far darker than any other spot. Any minute now, fireflies would begin sparking in the grass. From the old days, he remembered that his father always had at least one firefly night when the boys ran until after ten and enjoyed marshmallows around the fire pit behind the barn.

Did Liv still keep up that tradition? Probably. It appeared she'd kept everything else essentially the same without deviating much from what it had been like when Crockett was here.

And then the woman in question stepped out of her house and he was mesmerized. Her hair hung almost to her waist, out of the ponytail that she probably thought was practical but was still sexy as hell. If he let himself think about it. Which he wouldn't.

With the sun sinking lower and her hair flowing behind her, she looked like something mythical. She broke the spell when she zeroed in on him and frowned.

"Good, this saves me from having to come find you." She stalked toward him in the ugliest boots he'd ever seen. Taking her hair in hand, she twisted it into some kind of complicated knot and stuck a pen into the mass.

His hands clamped into a fist in his pockets to keep him from reaching for that pen.

"What do you want?" he said instead, reminding himself of Harold Beckham earlier today and how the words had been growled. And how he was still stuck here because he had failed to take care of the one situation Liv had brought to his attention in the five years he'd owned Breathe.

"You are coming with me, and we are going to check out that vandalism. You want to commit these boys to fixing something they didn't do, but just so you know, you—who didn't do anything either—will be out there too, wielding a brush and sweating right along with my boys."

She walked off toward a Jeep that had seen better days, obviously expecting him to follow along. When he didn't, she returned to yank him along behind her by the arm.

He wasn't a small man by any means, but Liv was strong for her size. Plus he was letting her get some of her aggression out. By allowing her to think she had the upper hand here, when he would have come if she had asked nicely as a suggestion, things might go better. But she didn't need to know that if it released some of her rage to feel in control.

"Do I need a flashlight, too?" he ventured to ask.

Her snarl was not comforting. "It's in the glove compartment."

He kept silent, hoping it would defuse her a bit. It didn't.

"I could have sworn you'd have more to say for yourself, or at least a little bit of gloating to do when you realized I was capitulating to this stupid plan."

"It's not capitulating if it's the right thing to do, Liv."

She whipped around so fast that the pen flew out from her haphazard bun and speared into the ground at his feet. Her hair fell around her shoulders and created a curtain for a moment before she pushed it off her face. He didn't remember ever having had such a strong urge to kiss a furious woman. This one came over him faster than anything ever had before.

Only strength of will and a complete sense of self-preservation kept him from following through on the urge. She'd bent over to retrieve the pen, and he didn't want it jabbed into his eye for taking liberties when she was so obviously pissed at him.

She stabbed the pen at the air in front of him before jamming it back into her tightly coiled hair. "This is so completely not the right thing to do. I firmly believe that these boys had nothing to do with this, and you should too. But you just whip out your checkbook and think that's going to make it all better. I asked you before, and I'll say it again, but didn't it occur to you, even once, that not one of those campers would have done anything to jeopardize their stay here? And when would they have had time?"

He certainly wasn't going to admit anything with her standing there like a Fury come to earth.

"Let's just get this over with and see how much work needs to be done before we argue any further." He walked away before he did something really stupid, like believe that the boys at the camp were coming out with the wrong end of the stick. He might have kept this camp open all these years, but it was only because of some misguided loyalty to his father, the one who cared more for the camp than for him and his mother. He was not going to put his neck out there for something that meant so little to him.

****

Taking a deep breath, Liv walked along behind Alex as he made his way around the barn in back of the Beckham house. She had almost seen red when he'd said this was the right thing to do. It felt so wrong as to be almost laughable, but she didn't have any other options.

While most of the townspeople believed in her kids, others seemed to treat this like it was a foregone conclusion that her boys—the kids she loved—had been the ones to do this terrible thing. She hadn't been allowed to see exactly how terrible after they had been accused, but words were enough to describe the picture. In her heart, she knew they just wouldn't have done anything to make them get into trouble, no matter what.

When she was confronted with the extent of the damage to the rear wall, her heart sank. It used all the right words and had the rounded and angled designs of inner-city graffiti, all right. But why would they have given themselves away like that? Why would they tag her neighbor's building and make it known they had such disdain for those who lived what was called the easy life?

Alex stood to the side, with one hand in his jeans pocket and the other flashing the light over the wall. He stood with a look of deep concentration on his face, his profile highlighted by the dying sun. She had to look away when the urge to bury herself in his strong arms nearly overwhelmed her. She couldn't believe the boys had betrayed her like this. And yet here was the proof, right in front of her eyes.

"We'll bring paint and ladders first thing tomorrow." She trudged off without another word, pain burning in her chest.

How could she have been so wrong?

She hadn't gone more than three steps when a firm grip stopped her, turning her around gently.

"Don't look so dejected, Liv. It's not that big a deal. We'll get it cleaned up, give the boys a lecture on how not to act out like this again, and then Beckham will drop the charges. You can go back to running your camp just the way you always have. Nothing has to change if you don't let it."

"Everything has." She felt like her eyeballs were floating in their sockets. They burned from holding back the tears of betrayal. From him, from the boys. What had she expected? She put her heart here, and it had been stomped on. Nothing new there.

Now, if she could just put one foot in front of the other and get back to the Jeep. She could go home, take a shower, lie down, and face this all tomorrow, maybe with a clearer head. Because right now, she couldn't take any more.

Like a miracle, though, Alex's strong arms came around her from behind and turned her into his chest. He was warm and smelled like the woods right after a good, soaking rain. His hard chest under her cheek felt like it could withstand the tide, much less the ebb and flow of her tears, so she gave in to them, sobbing as if her heart was broken, because it was.

****

She let him put her into the Jeep's passenger seat and handed over the keys with a docility that was totally unlike the Liv he'd come to expect from her emails and from being near her again. Alex felt helpless, and he didn't like it one bit.

But he drove them home, knowing better than to

try to engage her in conversation. His mother was the queen of the sulk. He had a lot of experience with that, at least.

He'd let her stew. She'd talk with him when she was ready and only when she was ready. In the meantime, he'd get her home, shut her into her cottage, and they'd talk tomorrow morning about how best to approach the campers.

He didn't know when he had made it his problem, too, but there it was. Probably about the time he saw the way this was tearing Liv up inside, though it shouldn't.

He rested a hand on her wrist where it lay on her thigh, squeezing when she didn't look at him. When she did finally look up, her tear-drenched eyes did him in. Without another thought, he pulled over to the side of the two-lane road, far enough onto the shoulder that they wouldn't get creamed, though there was no traffic at all on the road.

He pulled her into his arms without a moment's hesitation. She went willingly, burying her face in his chest. Her breath fanned through the material of his polo shirt and heated his skin. But he put down the instant image of her breath directly on his skin and concentrated on comforting her. He hadn't ever been this attached to the camp, so he couldn't fathom what she must be feeling. But something was ripping her up inside. Her beautiful eyes had been the windows to that pain a few moments ago.

They weren't in any rush to return home. The sun had set about an hour ago. With the onset of night, those fireflies had peeked out from their hiding places in the grasses around their feet back at the spray-painted barn. They, too, were long gone. He was alone with Liv out on this stretch of back road.

"Do you want to walk for a moment to get yourself back under control before we get back to the farm?"

"Don't be nice to me now, you might ruin your reputation." She pulled away from him, tucking herself up against the window with her arms wrapped securely around herself.

He fought hard not to meet her sarcasm with some of his own. But someone had to give first, and he was willing to do it this one time. "I just thought you might want to get some of your angst out before going back and possibly having to deal with something at Breathe. Bill told me you have a child who's having night terrors. I didn't know if you'd want him to see you like this if he chooses to have an episode tonight."

"You don't choose to have those kinds of 'episodes,' as you call them," she grumbled, but she got out of the car, and that had been his goal. It didn't matter how he attained it at this point.

He climbed out too and met her around the other side where the grass butted up against the shoulder of the road. Gravel crunched under their feet when they set off in the opposite direction of Breathe.

The silence was stark until an owl hooted above them. He hated to admit that he jumped, but he did, and it made Liv laugh a watery laugh.

"You really aren't a country boy anymore." She sniffed, and he wished he had a tissue for her. But she pulled one out of her pocket. That was his Liv, always prepared. Which was why her sobbing had taken him off his stride.

"Give me a wailing siren, or a loud argument next door, and I have no problem filtering it out, or not hearing it at all. All this silence is different, though. I can't seem to be comfortable here."

"You used to be fine here."

"That was a long time ago."

Her expression, what he could see with the full moon lighting the dark around them, shut down. The moon's rays limned her cheekbones. Definitely not the harsh light of a streetlamp like in Washington, DC, where the night could seem almost like the day in some areas.

"So are we going to the paint store tomorrow morning, or do we have supplies in storage for fixing our own property that we can use for Beckham?" He swung his arms in the humid night, letting the blood subside that had rushed through his body when he'd held her in the car. Slowly, it returned to the places it was supposed to be instead of the one place it, and his thoughts, shouldn't be. If he happened to brush her swinging arms every third step, well, she wasn't moving away, and neither was he.

"I'm sure we probably have everything in the storage shed that we might need, so don't worry about it coming out of your precious money just yet. Whatever we don't have, I plan on asking some of the people in town, and especially the ones who come out and volunteer their time, to help with. So, no worries."

He was tired of her always thinking he was looking at the bottom line and worrying about Breathe making him a profit. It rarely did. That was fine with him because it was a tax loss he could take every year.

That thought stopped him in his tracks. Maybe he was as bad as she said.

Still, he staunchly defended himself, not willing to

let her know how heartless he apparently could be. "It isn't the money. I just wanted to see if you needed anything while I was in town first thing tomorrow morning."

"Well, I don't. I wasn't planning on having you there when I explained this little setback to the boys anyway. They blame you already for not getting it taken care of. I haven't explained to them that you are only the silent partner. Some of them still remember Crockett and keep wishing you were him. That you would come in and teach them things. Be the father many of them don't have to the mother they've made me into."

He couldn't fathom it. And he wasn't falling for it. "I'm here to take care of the legal aspects and get things back under control so the camp can continue to run. I'm here to keep any of these kids from getting fined or sent home with a permanent record. I'm not here to be anyone's anything else but the money man."

She faced him, an expression of disbelief on her face. "You know, all these kids are looking for is to feel safe and to play like youth their age should be able to. They want to roam the countryside and feel the sunshine that isn't blocked by twenty-story buildings. Play in grass that isn't weed-choked or litter-filled. They want to be loved as many of them aren't. Some of them have good parents, but the majority of them are from foster homes or group homes, where they can't be more than a number because they'll move on again sometime soon."

He opened his mouth to say something—anything—to get her to stop, but she rode right over him.

"They want to walk outside and not worry about avoiding the drug dealers that want them to be customers or runners for their product. They want clean clothes and clean beds to sleep on. Three squares a day and maybe a treat from Bill if he's feeling in the Whoopie Pie mood. They aren't asking for much."

"And neither am I," he said when he could block the picture from his mind that she had painted. "I want to be able to go back to my own home and get back on track with my own life. I'll help you with this, and I'll write the checks, but like I said, I'm the money man."

"You don't have to tell me twice." She turned from him and headed back toward the car that was a good half mile away.

He let her go by herself this time. He needed a few moments to process what had just happened—and the thump in his chest when he'd realized that for a split second he did want to be Crockett. He did want to have twenty to thirty kids look at him as if he had the answers to all the questions the world threw at you. To have them trust him and want to be with him. Not because of the money he had, or the correct marriage match he could make, or the living he could provide. Not even for the financial advice he could offer or the clout he carried in the business world that could open doors for his friends and those who sometimes pursued him for that very thing. He wasn't some huge player in the political arena, but he knew people, people that other people wanted to know.

These kids just wanted to know what it was like to be safe and to have fun. To not hide because a gun could be pointing their way at any moment. They wanted to be fed and housed and clothed. They wanted to fit in as he had when he was younger. They wanted simple things, like a roof over their head and a place to call their own.

And Breathe was that home for at least a month out of the year. A month where they didn't have to worry about where their next meal was coming from because Bill had them covered. A month where laundry was clean, even if they had to do it. A month where they learned how to use a knife to whittle wood into ducks that were lopsided and would never sit right on a table. A month of sleeping on clean sheets and not having to hear people having sex in rooms close by or screaming at each other in a drunken blur.

And he could give them that, or at least make it possible, even if he didn't fully engage. Because as much as their plight struck him, he still wasn't willing to get completely involved. He would do the things he could, but that didn't include pretending that this was a place he loved. Those kids would see through him in a heartbeat.

Chapter Five

The sounds in Betty's diner, Petri's Dish, were muted at five-thirty in the morning on Tuesday. But she was big as life as Alex came into the establishment, dragging himself by sheer will up to the counter.

He hadn't slept well last night after sharing a silent car ride with Liv back to the farm. He hadn't slept well remembering the way her face had fit so snugly against his chest, the way her mere breath had set his whole body on high alert. She was his manager, he told himself over and over again. But he couldn't seem to make the message stick.

He'd only driven in this town once, when his father had died and Alex had come back for the funeral. Before that, his mother had taken him away at thirteen and hadn't let him ever come back. So he'd had to ask Bill for directions last night—after he'd tried to sneak back into the rambling farm house and had roused the older man from his bed by tripping over the runner in the front hall. After they'd pretty much scared the crap out of each other, Alex had explained what he needed and Bill had arranged it effortlessly, despite the fact that it was ten o'clock at night. He'd also given him a pair of jeans and a shirt, since Alex had no more clothes from his overnight bag and would be staying at least one more day.

And now, as the sun was just starting to come over

the horizon, and the air smelled fresh and clean, he'd stepped into the sizzle of grease on the grill and fried eggs. His stomach rumbled, regardless of the unearthly hour. He never got up this early at home. Never.

"There he is! I never thought I'd see my professional toast butterer again."

That voice and those words threw him back a step. That same voice had coaxed him through the aftermath of the fights his parents had fought within his hearing while thinking they were keeping their voices low enough to escape his notice. It had also soothed him when he'd had to leave, that last summer. She'd promised they'd see him again soon, despite the trouble. She told him she knew this because Crockett wouldn't let him stay away.

But he had stayed away for years, the longest stretch of time in the human experience, to a teenager.

The sounds of dishes clanking and coffee being poured splashed him back to the present when Betty came up and nearly lifted him off his feet with a bone-crushing hug. She only just topped five feet, but she sure packed a wallop. Carrying plates must have given her arms of steel. He suffered through the embrace for another moment before using his own strength to set her aside.

"You act like I've come back from the dead." He hadn't meant to say that.

And with good reason.

"Well, boy, I feared that might just be true."

He shrugged her words off. Betty had always been an exaggerator. The fish she caught was bigger than yours. Her stubbed toe trumped your broken leg.

"I'm here for reinforcements."

"Tell Betty what she can get you, and it's yours."

He pulled her aside and made her eyes pop with his request. Then he sat down at a booth and said hello to everyone who came in looking like he was a ghost. It hadn't been that long since he'd been here. Or maybe it had.

****

Rising from bed, Liv still wasn't sure how she was going to convince the boys that painting and fixing at the farm next door was a good idea. Even she didn't think it was a good idea, so how was she going to convince them?

If it had been a community project, then she could have put a positive spin on it. Or helping out a neighbor, she could have done that, too. But making them pay in work for something they hadn't done? She was stumped.

Hanging around her cottage and dragging her feet was not going to make the announcement any easier, though. She needed to just go in to breakfast, make the announcement, and then get them all moving. Like ripping off a bandage, worrying about how much it was going to hurt had to be worse than it would be when she finally gathered the courage to do it.

Throwing on capri pants and a camp T-shirt, she slipped her feet into tennis shoes and drew her hair back into a ponytail. She went without makeup because she didn't want to sweat it off in the baking sun. The local radio station had called for record temperatures today, of course.

Beckham wanted sweat? He'd get sweat, just as soon as she convinced the boys that they wanted to do this, not that they had to.

Taking a deep breath, she walked into the dining room, where over forty people sat eating French toast and cheesy hash browns. More than twenty of them were adults, including several teenagers, from town. What on earth was going on here?

"Have some breakfast," Uncle Bill said, handing her a plate and leading her to a seat.

"Why are all these people here?" she whispered out of the side if her mouth.

"To help. Alex has been busy. Just be thankful when he tells you. Don't bring out the hissy fit I can see brewing in your eyes."

She knew it was there and tried to tamp it down. What had he done? This was her camp and her campers. Had he told them? How had he told them? What had he told them?

He'd better not have lied. That was one of her biggest rules. The truth, always, even if it wasn't easy.

The buzz in the dining hall picked back up now that she was seated. Alex came over with a grin on his face. She smiled back for good measure, even if she didn't feel it reach her eyes.

"We're due over at the Beckham Farm in thirty minutes, so you might want to eat a little faster," he said as he took the chair next to hers.

She shoveled some cheesy hash browns into her mouth to keep herself from asking him what exactly he had done.

"I gathered everyone I could from the diner this morning, and Betty said she would send more over once they arrived for breakfast." His smile got wider, and she shoved more food into her mouth. At this rate, she was going to look like a chipmunk and be sick to her stomach. She forced herself to swallow and took a sip of orange juice.

"We should have a pretty good showing, from what Betty said. We'll have this thing done in no time. The classes you were going to postpone are scheduled for later in the day. Bill gave me the schedule, and I called everyone to see if they could help out and then come here a little later in the day."

And didn't she just feel ineffective? He'd been gone for years, never been a real part of this camp, and within twenty-four hours he'd taken it all over as if he'd been doing it for years. He was Crockett's son to the core. She should have remembered that when she called him. Now it wasn't anger bubbling in her throat, it was tears.

"What? No 'thank you'? Nothing to say? I thought you'd be pleased."

"Pleased as punch." Bill shot her a look at the tone in her voice. "Thank you," she said with less snarkiness. "May I speak with you outside for a moment?"

"Of course. Or you can do it between bites. We really do need to get going to keep to the schedule I set up." He glanced at his watch, and she gripped her fork tighter.

"It won't take long," she ground out between clenched teeth.

Not that he noticed, of course.

Popping a last piece of French toast into her mouth, she dabbed her lips with a napkin while mentally composing all the things she wanted to say but wouldn't. If she got them all out of the way in her mind, then maybe there would be less chance of them spewing out at high volume.

He followed her out the side door with his hands tucked into the pockets of his jeans and a bounce in his step. His shirt was a soft blue, button-down, collared shirt that looked familiar, but she supposed it could have just been something he brought with him.

Perky thing, wasn't he? Now that he'd come in and saved the freaking day.

She turned on him as soon as she heard the door click closed behind him.

"What did you say to them? How did you get them to agree to this? You better not have lied, or so help me God, I will take it out of your hide!"

He raised his hands as if in surrender. Again, she thought he would never surrender without a backup plan. And she wasn't wrong.

"I did not lie."

She snorted. "You told them the farmer refuses to believe it was anyone but them, and this is their punishment, and they just merrily went along with it? I highly doubt that. I know my boys. They would be furious at the injustice."

"Actually, they weren't." Rocking back on his heels, he didn't smile this time. Instead he narrowed his eyes at her. "I think you underestimate them and want to give them more than they are actually expecting here. You want this place to be a mythical fairytale, or like a fantasyland where nothing bad happens. But even in the non-ghetto world things aren't always fair. Sometimes you have to do what's good instead of fighting for what's right."

"I know that." Of course she did.

"Then stop trying to make this place so unlike

where they come from. The letdown of going home from the most perfect place back to your miserable home has to be a huge adjustment. Yes, they want safe and clean, and yes, that's different from home for some of them. But some come from good homes and do this so their moms have one less mouth to feed over the summer."

Now she was the one rocking back, and not just on her heels. She almost fell on her ass.

****

Alex made a grab for Liv's elbow when it appeared she might fall. "Liv?"

"I'm fine, just stumbled." She stepped back quickly, shaking him off. "Thanks for everything you did. I'm going to go get ready, and I'll be back so I'm on time for the trip to the farm."

"We have a few minutes. Aren't you going to finish your breakfast?" But he was talking to her retreating back.

Bill stood next to him a moment later. "She's just excited, I'm sure. The work will be done quickly, and then things will go back to normal."

"She didn't look excited." In his opinion, she'd looked devastated. She hadn't wanted the boys to do the work in the first place. He got it. But at least this would clear up the mess, both physically and legally. He couldn't be sorry for that.

She'd asked him to come to Breathe and he had. He'd fixed the issue, as she'd asked, and the legal aspect was over. Maybe he could go home tomorrow.

Should he go after her? As he turned to Bill to ask as they entered the dining room, the older man shook his head with his lips clamped tight.

And then she entered the room again, a big smile on her face and her hair pulled up into a high ponytail.

"Okay, let's get moving so we can get this all done. The sooner we're there, the sooner we're done and you can get to the cheesecake lesson."

Every boy rose from his chair with his tray. They formed a line to clean their dishes off and then deposited their plates in a gray tub. Alex didn't know who cleaned those dishes from there, but he was happy it wasn't him.

Each guy went past Liv and patted her on the shoulder. She stood straight and smiled at all of them. The taller ones patted her on the head, and the last one stopped to tell her they understood and weren't pissed about it. Things happened.

The smile remained until she was looking at the last boy's back. And then the shoulders drooped and the smile fell. It was only for a moment. Alex would have missed it if he hadn't been watching her so closely. But he had been looking, and he was still looking when she straightened back up and met his gaze.

After one brief look, she walked past him without a word.

The words he'd said to her, the way he'd told her the kids weren't looking for some kind of fairytale, struck him as unfair when he re-examined the exchange. She believed in them and in everything she did for them. He remembered she'd been brought from a bad situation when she was younger. This had probably been like heaven to her after living on and off the streets. Most likely, she only wanted to recreate what she'd felt. He'd ripped that away from her with a few well-meant words.

Without truly knowing if they'd done anything, he'd consigned these kids to fix-it hell. And he'd done it all while telling her that her dream of what this place represented wasn't right. He felt like shit.

The repairs were going to take more than a few days, so he was staying. Hopefully Bill had some more clothes he could borrow, though Alex was surprised they fit. He and Bill were not similar in size, to say the least.

Maybe while he was here he could make it up to the boys without actually appearing to do so. And if that helped Liv, then it would be just a bonus. Because by giving in without a fight, he might have just put a very large black mark on Breathe's reputation, the one thing that had mattered the most to his dad, the thing Alex had been handed and told to take care of. And it would not look good to have this place thought of as bad or poorly run. Damn.

Twenty minutes later, they went to work. Armed with buckets, paint cans, brushes, and truckloads of wood and supplies, it seemed as if the whole town showed up at the Beckham farm to set up shop. Alex had never seen the town come together like this before. Reassuring hands were set on shoulders of the Breathe boys. Congratulations and high fives were exchanged when they finally were able to remove the lingering pieces of particularly vulgar and bright words that had been spray-painted onto the side of the barn. One boy, Johnny, knew the best way to get the paint to come off more easily and how much primer to use before using the paint to touch it up.

Johnny's brother had been a tagger for years, until he had been killed in a drive-by shooting. Johnny had taken pictures of all his brother's handiwork around the city before he'd set out with his removing solvent and primer to take down the things his brother had done in his short life. But he had then replaced several with murals that he'd created himself, depicting a better place and time. Now Mr. Beckham let him paint, on a barn door, a scene with a tractor in a field, and then a second one when it was obvious the kid had talent.

Other kids were adept at nailing new boards in place, or at least they were after they were assisted and taught by one of the carpenters Alex had looked up this morning at six, with Betty's blessing. Her son was one of the ones currently helping a teen make sure the board was lined up precisely before putting any nails in.

And through the whole thing, Alex helped, but he still held himself apart just a little. This was not his town, it wasn't his home. It wasn't his community, no matter how much he had spouted earlier in the café to get people to help. Because he still couldn't shake the feeling that he didn't belong now, as he hadn't belonged then.

No one in particular made him feel that way, but there was something inside himself that wouldn't let him relax here in this backwoods town that his father had loved more than anything, even his family.

****

Liv hosted a huge dinner back at Breathe after the long day of repairs and the rescheduled workshops. They still had a lot to do, but they were well on their way to fixing what was damaged. Now if they could just find the animals.

Bill had been exuberant at the chance to make even bigger meals than normal. He'd been a warrant officer in the mess in the Navy, and it was like the old days for him to serve more than twenty at a time. He was in heaven.

"Are you sure we have enough of everything?" Liv asked, snitching a carrot from the bowl of water on the island in the center of the kitchen.

"If you'll stop taking a bite out of everything, I'm sure we'll be fine. Now get out of here and go make sure the tables all have linens. Marcy and I will be fine in here. I've fed as many as three hundred full-grown seagoing men at a time, and I can handle this crowd with my eyes closed."

Liv shared a raised eyebrow with Marcy, who also shrugged and laughed before Liv headed out. Liv didn't know what she would do without those two in the kitchen. Sure, she could make a mean baked chicken and knew how to whip up some mashed potatoes that would make your mouth water, but she had never aspired to be like her uncle in the kitchen. Running Breathe had always been her dream, and she'd been living it for the last five years with minimal input from her boss.

Part of her hoped things would go back soon to the way they were, now that the threat of trouble was over.

But the other part of her had watched Alex interact with the boys today and was overwhelmed by the feeling of rightness in working side by side with him and the majority of the town. That was how Crockett had imagined things for the camp after he had been ready to hand over the reins. Instead, he'd died too early, and his son had never taken an interest and in fact had been much the opposite.

But now that Alex was back, she didn't know what

63

to think. Being in his arms had been a little bit of heaven and a lot of hell last night. It had been a long time since she'd been held by a man. Her son gave the best hugs, but being in Alex's arms was a whole different experience.

And seeing the way he could really interact with the people in town when he let himself unbend was a miracle in and of itself. He'd gotten people to do things she didn't think even she could have done. And they'd all smiled and asked what else he needed. It was like having Crockett here all over again.

Though she'd never say that to Alex, because he would probably run faster than she could say, "Sorry."

But he was like Crockett nonetheless, except he was far more handsome and made her think about things she hadn't thought of in years. A home, more children of her own, a life with a partner who would work beside her and love her. She'd thought she'd had that with Paul, but then he died and left her to fend for herself with a baby on the way. Crockett and Bill had been godsends in helping raise her little boy, and now he sat at a long table with his friends for the summer.

She waved to him discreetly, as he didn't always like everyone to know that she was his mother. It had caused some kids to be mean to him last year. This year most of the kids knew, but he wasn't talking about it. And he wasn't taking special privileges. He was just one of the camp boys and had worked just as hard if not harder out there today at the barn. She couldn't be more proud if she tried.

Turning to the left, she changed her focus to Alex from her spot at the slightly ajar door into the dining room. He made the rounds of the area, shaking hands and smiling. He looked like he had the world at his feet, or at least the town of Langston.

A feeling of hope took over as she turned to Bill, and she looked him up and down. She remembered where she'd seen that shirt. "Did you give Alex some of Crockett's clothes?"

"Yes."

"Did you tell him they were his father's jeans and shirt?"

"No."

"Did he ask?" she pressed.

"No."

Liv sighed. She wouldn't say anything either. No wonder he looked more like Crockett. But where she had thought of Crockett as a father figure, she couldn't help but admire his son as a man.

Her friend Maddie spotted her and came bustling over as quickly as her very pregnant body would allow. Liv thought for a second about ducking out, knowing Maddie would never be able to catch her, but it would only put off the inevitable.

"Why aren't you out here, honey? This is your party, too!" Maddie dragged her by the arm into the center of the room, right next to Alex. Alex, who had recently showered after their hard day of labor and wore another familiar shirt. He smelled like clean, fresh soap and a light cologne that nearly had her snuffling his neck to get a better whiff. She was horrified when she realized the path of her thoughts. That would not only be way beyond professional, it would also be way more than anyone here needed to see.

She took a step away, just a little one, but enough that the distance allowed her to breathe without pulling him into her lungs.

The reprieve only lasted a moment as he grabbed her elbow and pulled her into his side where he slung his arm around her shoulders.

"A round of applause for the true heroine of today. She never had a doubt and I shouldn't have either. And she slaps on a mean coat of paint."

Cheers broke out across the room, rolling around and through her until she thought she'd cry. This was her home, her people, her life. And since when was she so weepy?

She playfully shoved away from the nearness of Alex. At least she hoped it had looked playful. Bowing to him, she then bowed to the audience surrounding her. What had he meant about how he shouldn't have doubted?

"In reality, it's the boys who have done so much. And with the help of our friends and neighbors, we were able to get most of it done today. The rest will go in next week, and then it will be as good as new. Better than new!" she answered.

"I want to say something," a gruff voice called over the cheering. A gap in the crowd formed for Harold Beckham to come stomping forward in his overalls and flannel shirt. His sparse hair was neatly combed over his bald head from right to left, and his John Deere cap was in his hands.

When he made it to the front where Liv stood with Alex, he got right in between them and clamped a hand on each of their shoulders. Liv felt the weight of his hand like a benediction. They had done something good and real today, because it was a punishment, yes, and it was expected. But she knew in her heart that these boys would have done it only because it was needed if they'd been given a chance. She couldn't have taught this lesson any better.

"This boy and this woman are two of the luckiest people on the face of God's green earth, second only to these hard-working boys. I wanted to say I was sorry for doubting and to tell you that I'm donating a good portion to your cause as well as being willing to entertain taking on a farm hand or two if any of you are interested. Despite this bit of trouble, I'm actually not a really bad guy."

That was probably more words than she had ever heard from the old guy, all strung together. And it was an opportunity she had hoped to have at one time. As more of these boys were getting older, she wanted them to be able to have choices, ways they could move out of their neighborhoods and into hers. Eventually, they might go back to their own towns and make a difference there with a solid foundation for adulthood.

She'd have to get together with Alex to see how they could do this. They hadn't talked about him staying for longer, even though all the work wasn't done yet.

Provided he would still be here tomorrow morning, maybe they could actually discuss this face to face instead of over email. It would be a novelty—as long as she could keep herself from sniffing at him like a dog.

Chapter Six

The house was shut up tight and all fourteen bedrooms upstairs were filled with contented snores and little huffs that signaled a hard day's work was being followed by needed rest in snoozeland. Alex wandered down the hall, making sure that everything was as it should be. He'd taken the shift from Bill to give the older man some much-deserved sleep of his own. He'd fed them this afternoon, bringing sandwiches to the other farm for everyone there, and then this evening's meal of spaghetti and meatballs with salad and French bread had outdone even that. Alex was pretty sure he was going to be at least ten pounds heavier when he left.

Which should be tomorrow. He had no more clothes. He could probably get more from Bill, but he'd looked at the collar of the shirt before he put it on this afternoon and he'd seen the initials C.C.

He was wearing his father's clothes and wading knee deep in his father's dream. This was not what he had come here for.

He sighed and leaned against the upstairs hall wall. He wasn't ready to go just yet, though, and he didn't know why. He had a ton of things he could be doing at home, including social engagements that he'd put off, outings with friends and his mother that he had rescheduled to come out here and clean up this mess.

But now that it was mostly cleaned, he didn't want to go just yet. And that made him feel extremely conflicted inside. He should stay and see this all the way through. They might need him.

Shoving away from the wall, he made himself do the rest of the circuit of the upstairs, then went outside to the back patio to get a breath of fresh air. The moon rode low in the sky, and fireflies lit the blades of soft grass. He toed off his shoes, then pulled off his socks. Barefoot, he took a walk in the soft, springy turf, just letting the cares of the day fade.

He'd made some mistakes while he was here, ones that he'd like to overcome before he left. He'd also done things to celebrate, triumphs that would stay with him for the rest of his life.

Maybe he could stay for just another few days to help finish it out. In the meantime, he'd also be able to amass a few more of these memories. Nothing was so important back in DC that he couldn't hold it off until next weekend. There was nothing on his plate that needed his immediate attention. So maybe he'd take the time. And in that time maybe he'd send out some inquiries to find out who had actually done the damage, and take the tarnish off Breathe and off Liv as the director. It was the least he could do.

With his toes sunk into the soft grass, he leaned against the corral at the side of the barn and watched a filly and her colt do one more lap of the exercise yard before being called in by one of the hands. There was a freedom in the horses, a way of life that had always eluded him.

And he was being morose in the moonlight. They had all celebrated tonight, but he felt like riding this feeling to its fullest. And to best do that, he should go get Liv and see if she wanted to take a drive, maybe go to the ice cream shop he'd seen in town. It was old-time style with a soda jerk behind the counter and tall, red leather stools pulled up to the counter.

He'd noticed it earlier because it used to be a candy shop when he'd lived here. He'd taken his three dollars a week allowance and had splurged it all on penny candy when his mother would take him into town on Sunday afternoons.

He hadn't remembered that when he'd seen it, but now the memory lived clearly in his mind. His mother and he would set off in her station wagon, driving down the long road leading into town. He'd look back over his shoulder wishing his summer friends could come with him. And his mother would tell him to turn around and enjoy this time alone with her without twenty other kids taking up all her time.

A nicker close by brought his mind back to the present. The young horse butted its head against his hand where he had his arms crossed on the fence. Its nose was velvety softness under his fingers. Briefly, he wondered if Liv's skin would be that soft. He'd shut the thought out all day since he had seen her across the yard at Beckham's farm with paint on her nose and her hair flying away from her braid. She'd lifted her elbow up to use her forearm to push back her hair, and he wondered if her skin was soft just there under her jaw.

Dangerous thoughts to have as her boss, but it was only in his mind, so they weren't that dangerous. Plus, he would be gone in a matter of days, and they would return to their emails and infrequent phone calls.

With his hand still stroking the horse, he turned

and noticed that the front light in her cottage was on. Maybe he shouldn't ask her out to ice cream. As innocent as it all might be, he didn't want to do anything to jeopardize what he had here.

But then the choice wasn't an easy one when she came out of her house wearing a pair of shorts with no shoes, and the miles of her endless legs glinted in the faint light cast by the moon. They would surely be smooth. So smooth his fingers literally itched to touch them. So he stuck his hands in his pockets and greeted her as if he didn't have a million completely inappropriate thoughts running rampant through his fertile and too-long-celibate mind.

"Can't sleep again?" she asked, her arms crossed under her chest as she leaned a hip against the railing surrounding the corral.

"Nah, I'm just enjoying the quiet before I go in. Big day today."

"Yep, big day. I didn't thank you properly before, for all you did for the boys."

He turned from the fence and leaned back into it with his hands still in his pockets. The urge to touch her hadn't yet passed, and he wasn't going to tempt himself.

But then she leaned next to him and placed her hand on his forearm. "Thank you so much for helping and for showing them that it's human to be wrong and even better to admit it. I know they didn't do this, but you were right that it didn't hurt them to fix it."

He couldn't resist covering her hand with his and testing whether she really was as soft as she looked. Not surprisingly, she was. And he had never felt so close to someone with so little contact.

Her smile was uncertain in the light of the moon when he moved his hand to her cheek. But she leaned into his caress for just the briefest of moments before she pulled back with a frown on her face.

"Anyway, thanks for everything today." She took a step back and put her hands behind her. "I appreciate it. So does this mean you're out of here tomorrow? I don't think you really need to stay here at this point, with everything done. I mean everything that you came here for, anyway."

She was rambling, and he didn't know why. But he was going to shoot down her idea for him to leave right now, against his better judgment.

"I have the time and I'm already here, so I figure I'll just hang out for a little while longer. At least until next week, so I can help finish up the project and see it through with the boys. I don't feel right leaving with it half done. I have some things I'd like to look into for the farm, too, and it will be easier in person."

Her face went through so many emotional changes in a few seconds that he didn't know if he'd read her correctly. Not to mention that it was getting darker by the minute, so it was hard to discern what exactly he'd seen.

"Suit yourself. You can see how the boys do out here in the wild blue. I'm sure Crockett is smiling, up in heaven, that you're finally here again."

****

And what was she going to do now? Liv thought as she stood in the lowering darkness with Alex. Leaning into his hand on her cheek earlier had been a mistake, a temptation she hadn't resisted. But she'd thought he'd be gone first thing tomorrow morning, and now he'd be here for days yet.

She didn't run away from him as she wanted to, didn't escape to the confines and comfort of her little cottage that stood no more than twenty feet away. She wasn't a coward. But there was a part of her that wished she was there right now and hadn't followed the allure of seeing him silhouetted against the backdrop of the pasture, looking good enough to tackle.

Instead, she continued to stand there hoping for something, though her heart wanted one thing and her mind wanted another. Neither was going to get their desire.

Her mind wanted him to go ahead and go back to Washington, DC so they could once again get on even footing, with him checking in every once in a great while to make sure she didn't need anything. And her heart wanted him to stay, knowing now what it was like to work and play with the man who had grown from the boy she had started to care about before he went away.

Paul had tried, when they were married, but he'd been a truck driver, too restless to stay in one place too long. She had to believe that Alex wanted to run back to his own life as soon as possible. It was that or dream impossible dreams. Damn.

When the stars started popping out in the night sky, she tilted her head up to get a good look and to avoid his gaze that seemed to be probing hers.

"So you don't have anything to say about me being here longer, other than that Crockett would like it?"

"What do you expect me to say?"

"I'm not sure, but I thought you'd have a problem with me horning in on your parade. Or thinking that I'm hanging the boss thing over your head." He laughed, but it didn't reach his eyes. The outside lights had come on with the dark and illuminated him in soft yellow light. She could see his face now, and if she had to guess she'd say he was anxious. But what did he have to be anxious about? After all, it was his place, and she just ran it.

"I don't have a problem with you being here at all." She shrugged, though she didn't feel nonchalant in the least. It would be awkward with him here, especially since this was bound to send her Uncle Bill over the moon. Then Alex would bring down the hammer when he left and shatter Bill's illusions that Alex was finally interested in the farm and Breathe.

The more she thought about it, the worse the idea sounded. But she couldn't back out of her yes now.

"I'm sure it will be fine to have you here, and I can actually go over the accounts with you face to face now. We can get some work done while you're here, if you're up to it, and then you won't have to worry about us the rest of the year, if you don't want to."

His face fell into a frown. "I don't worry about you at all. Crockett knew what he was doing when he set you up as the director. You've done a great job."

"Thanks for that. And before my head gets too big, I should probably go in and get some sleep. I'm sure the boys will be up early and rambunctious tomorrow morning after all the fresh air today. I guess I'll head in."

"How about going out for some ice cream with me to celebrate? It's too early to turn in yet, and I'd like to take you out to thank you for everything you do. These are good kids. My treat."

She couldn't do anything but accept. He was the

boss, after all. But the silent part of her wondered what in the heck she was getting herself into when she hadn't been out in over eight years with anyone, and the first invitation she got and accepted was from her boss. She'd always thought she was smart, but when she said yes, she started rethinking if that were actually true anymore.

Maybe she should have her head examined for going out with him. Yet it didn't stop her from going back into her cottage after promising him she'd be back in ten minutes. Nor did it stop her from primping just a little in front of her bathroom mirror—fluffing out her ponytail a little bit, even though she wanted to take it out altogether, putting on lip gloss and wishing it was lipstick. She stopped herself before she changed her clothes, thankfully.

This was just a simple thank-you ice cream, nothing to be worried about. Nothing to feel insecure about. And certainly nothing to place any importance on. He probably took his business associates out to high-priced dinners all the time, wining and dining the people who made up his various businesses, his managers at each place. Why not her?

But she couldn't help thinking, just for a moment, that those other managers were more sophisticated than she was and knew the rules. She had no idea and hoped that her ignorance wasn't going to lead her down some slippery slope that she wouldn't be able to climb back up.

Before she could talk herself out of going, she left the cottage and met Alex in front of the house. She'd thought they would take the Jeep since it was the property of the farm, but he was standing outside his low-slung sports car.

At least he didn't open the door for her. That would have been one step too close to a real date.

Liv had never been in a car this expensive or this luxurious before. Her little sedan got her around when she needed to run errands by herself. The Jeep took her out in the terrain as needed. The minivan that belonged to Breathe got her around with a few boys in the back if they had doctor appointments or things that had to be done with a few but not all. And the bus was great for carting them all around if they were going on a field trip to Indian Echo Caverns or taking the day to go to the aquarium.

But this leather interior was nothing like the hard vinyl of all those vehicles. The seats in those did not cuddle her backside the way this seat did. They didn't make her feel like she could blissfully and gratefully sink in and sleep for the next few hours without a single crick in her neck.

Trying not to look like a rube, she subtly stroked the leather a few times, hoping Alex couldn't see her in the dark interior. How mortifying would that be?

"There's this place over near the diner, and it looks like it might be new." He laughed as he shifted the car into a higher gear. "But what do I know? Anything less than twenty years old looks new to me at this point."

He laughed again, but it sounded a little strained to her ears. She dismissed it as her own sensitivity to the whole situation.

Living in a small town like she did meant that no trip was as long as you wanted it to be when you were riding in such a snazzy car. Before she knew it they were on Front Street and Alex was searching for a parking spot. One opened right in front of the ice cream shop. It was a parallel spot. She figured he had to do this all the time in the city, so she didn't worry about his skills until he put his arm across the back of her seat to better position himself to see where he was parking.

Her breathing pattern shortened until she forcefully slowed it down. He was so masculine, so there, and the scent of his cologne wafted through the air conditioning to her, drawing her nearer. He smiled at her as his head tilted front and back to make sure he was parking correctly and each time he glanced her way.

What had she ever done to deserve this? She couldn't get out of the car fast enough once he was done parking. His smile was still in place when he met her on the sidewalk, but she felt a little wobbly. His hand under her elbow was welcome and yet did nothing for her equilibrium.

She breathed a sigh of relief (or was that disappointment?) when he dropped his hand after opening the door for her, and the frigid air inside the shop hit her face. It was certainly cool enough in here. She just hoped she wasn't blushing, because there was no heat in the place to explain away any tint of red to her face.

****

"This is nice," Alex said, licking around his cone and hoping that Liv was enjoying her malted milk shake. He'd tried to talk her into a double dip, but she wouldn't go for it. He didn't blame her once he saw how big the thing was in his waffle cone.

She slurped and swallowed. "It is. I appreciate you bringing me out. I haven't been here in a while, and it's nice to be out without twenty other people demanding your time and attention."

"Yeah, it must get old, but you seem to handle it really well."

"Thanks, I think."

"That didn't come out right." His brow crinkled. "What I meant was that it takes a special kind of person to be able to deal with that many kids and still be sane. My dad was that kind of person and so are you."

"Nice save."

"You liked that?"

She couldn't help but laugh at his cheekiness. "I did, though it doesn't exactly change the fact that you were being a bonehead at the beginning."

He licked more of his cone, and she waited for him to be finished before she said, "So what do you see yourself doing while you're here?" She did not want him underfoot and second-guessing her decisions. Not to mention the fact that he would now be here during her annual cook-off.

The event was going to be stressful enough without worrying about him being here and judging what she did and how she did it. Normally she just sent him an update following the event, with how much had been raised and her plans for what she would do with the money.

Now he would be there for the whole thing, and she wasn't sure she liked that at all. Maybe she could just not invite him. A novel idea, but one that she would not be able to get past Bill, who would be so happy that Alex was staying, once he found out. This was not how she had planned to spend her summer. Then again, she was a survivor, and it wasn't that long for her to get through.

She'd seen and done worse before.

He twirled his spoon into and around the top of the waffle cone. "Isn't the cook-off coming up? I could help with that."

"No, thanks."

His raised eyebrow was no doubt in response to her not-so-slow and not-so-nice answer. Darn it, now she probably had to explain herself. It wasn't that hard, though. He just couldn't help. It was as simple as that. But she'd have to be diplomatic.

"I have enough helping hands already, and very few things left to do. It would be better if we just kept it as is for right now. Hey, maybe if you like it, you could come back for next year and help with that one." Like that was ever going to happen, but she felt like she ought to at least throw him a bone.

"I doubt I'll be here for the next one."

That's what she'd thought. "Well, you could always come to this one and just enjoy yourself. No work involved, just all fun, all the time. I'm sure it's been a while since you've played."

He seemed to think about that for a moment, staring into her eyes while he downed the last three bites of his cone. She'd never enjoyed an ice cream more, nor had she ever suffered through it so much. Her hormones must have been going wacky, because this was her boss and he was completely off limits. Yet she couldn't shake the feeling that she envied that ice cream. Ridiculous. Absolutely ridiculous. And she had to get out of here before she did something even more ridiculous.

"We should head back." She slurped the last of her milk shake, turned, and threw the paper cup into the trash can. "I don't normally leave Bill all alone with the kids. It's too much for him."

He followed her from the ice cream shop, close on her heels to open the door before she could.

"Thanks," she said at the same time he said, "So you have no social life throughout the whole summer?"

Try the whole year, she thought, but she certainly wasn't going to tell him that.

"It's all worth it. I love the kids. We're doing important work here, and it fulfills me." Would he realize she hadn't answered his question?

He opened the door to the car, and she gratefully sank into the leather seat again. They were quiet on the way home, but it was a good quiet, a comfortable one. And yet again they were home way too fast.

He didn't have to walk her to her door, but he did anyway. This could get awkward fast, she thought, until she reminded herself that they'd just had business ice cream and not a date. He'd opened the shop door for her and the car door for her. Like a gentleman. That was all. They hadn't held hands or even really talked about anything except business. She was safe.

Stepping up on her tiny front porch, Alex waited while she fumbled her key out of her pocket and missed twice while trying to insert it into the lock.

"Need help?"

Yeah, maybe the mental kind. Her hands were shaking for no good reason. Taking a discreet deep breath, she tried again, then turned to him to say goodnight.

"It was fun. Thanks for all the help today," she said quickly.

"You know, I actually had far more fun than I

thought I would, today *and* tonight. I owe that all to you."

She shrugged. "It happens if you stay around long enough." She laughed to cover up her nervousness.

"I don't doubt it now." His voice dropped to a husky tone as he moved toward her, his gaze dropping to her lips. When he cupped her cheek for the second time that day, she found herself rooted to the spot. He sealed his lips to hers in a kiss that stole her breath, even as her eyes remained wide open. They didn't stay that way for long. Her eyelids drifted down as she got lost in the way he mastered the kiss, running his hand along her shoulder and wrapping his other arm around her waist. It wasn't a demanding kiss. It was soft and exploratory, his lips whispering over hers. And when he opened his mouth, so did she.

She should stop this, she really should, but not just yet. For the moment she was caught up in being kissed like she'd never been kissed before.

The sound of running feet had her jerking back from Alex. Looking over his shoulder, she saw Davey heading her way, his arms churning and his bare feet pounding fast across the grass.

"Mom, Mom! Uncle Bill told me to come get you! Manny's having another one of his night screams. Come quick!"

She risked a glance at Alex and found him staring down at the little boy who didn't resemble her very much. Davey took after his father's side of the family. It had been a running joke that she did all the work and he got all the credit. If Alex knew about her boy, he'd never asked after him. When he'd arrived, she'd chosen not to point him out.

And if Alex didn't know about Davey, then it was none of his business. She didn't talk about her son in their brief exchanges. They stayed strictly on an employee/employer plane and had for years. Except, that kiss…

Alex ran a hand over his mouth as if wiping her away. Her breath hitched, but there wasn't much she could do at the moment. She had a frightened boy to soothe.

Taking off at a brisk walk, she kept pace with Davey, whose mouth ran a mile a minute.

"And then he sat up and just started screaming, but no one can get him to stop, and we didn't want to wake him up in case it gets worse, and Uncle Bill tried to do everything he could, but he told me to come get you, so I did."

"Thank you, Davey. I appreciate it. We'll get Manny calmed down. You did good work."

They entered the house through the back and took the stairs right off the kitchen to the second floor. She could hear the crying, and it broke her heart. She'd done research after the first episode and hoped the techniques she'd learned would work this time.

"What can I do to help?" Alex said, walking briskly right beside her. She hadn't realized he had followed them because she'd been concentrating so hard on what Davey was saying and on what to do for Manny. The look in Alex's eyes told her he wanted some answers but that he would wait until the current crisis was over.

At least there was that.

Chapter Seven

The child sat on the bed, his eyes open but unseeing as he whimpered, then screamed, then whimpered again. Alex had never seen anything like it.

"How long has this been going on?" Liv asked, sitting on the edge of the boy's bed. She was surrounded by twenty kids in all shapes, sizes, and ages. And every single one of them had a worried look on his face. Even her own kid, who went to a bunk and pulled a blanket off, along with a teddy bear, and brought them back to his mom. His mom. How had he not known that she had a child? Was he hers? Had she adopted?

His curly hair didn't match hers, and his dark, dark eyes weren't shaped like hers, but perhaps he favored the father. The father who was where? She couldn't be married. She would never have let him kiss her if she were married. Was it a relationship gone wrong? Or maybe she was a widow? Maybe she had the child out of wedlock.

Somewhere in the very back of his mind he very vaguely remembered Crockett mentioning a new addition to the farm from Liv, but then he'd never mentioned it again. It could have had something to do with the fact that while Alex couldn't remember the mention, he very clearly remembered telling the old man that he didn't need to know what happened out at the farm because it had nothing to do with him.

There had been a long silence before his father had hung up, and then the calls had tapered off. Crockett had still called every month, but sometimes Alex took the call and sometimes he didn't. The last call he should have taken but didn't was the week before Crockett had died.

Alex shoved the thought aside. All that would have to wait while he assisted in any way he could. "What can I do?"

Davey handed Liv the teddy bear and the blanket while Alex stood there feeling useless. Probably the same thing every other person in this room was feeling while the boy on the bed cried and screamed. The younger ones flinched when he hit a certain pitch. And Alex knew how he could help.

"Let's give Miss Olivia some room. I know a secret place Crockett used to take me to look at the stars when I was very good. If you haven't been there, we should go." He hoped that the platform was still there. If it wasn't, he would come up with something else.

With a line of boys behind him, he went from the second floor to the third floor. There was a door somewhere here, if only he could remember where. He closed his eyes for a moment, trying to recall his father leading him up here years ago after his mother was asleep. She didn't like him to be up so high and thought it was ridiculous to go to the roof when they could see the stars perfectly well from the front yard.

And then he remembered. At the back of the house, right under the stairs to the attic, next to the original chimney someone had folded in on itself instead of removing it when it was no longer in use. Alex used to wonder what was in it and imagine animals living there, making nests and hiding away when it got cold outside.

He led the group to the door, hoping it hadn't been barred or that he'd need a key of some sort. But the handle turned under his hand, and he took a moment to make sure it would remain unlocked from this side so they didn't get stuck outside. It was a widow's walk, even though there was no ocean for as far as the eye could see. Traditionally, a widow's walk was so the women of days gone by could watch for their men coming home after a journey. This one was for decoration—and for him and his father to stargaze.

"Stay back for a moment and let me make sure the boards are all sound. The last thing we need is someone falling through the floor."

He heard a whimper behind him and cursed himself for putting that image into one of the boys' heads. He was not cut out for this, but he was trying his damnedest to do the right thing.

It was as if no time had passed when he stepped out onto the platform. The railing was intact, the boards solid and firm, and the sky glorious above him.

"Okay, you can come out." He counted seventeen heads as they came through the door to stand with him. There should have been eighteen, even though Davey had stayed behind with his mom.

Keeping an eye on the ones with their faces raised to the sky, Alex went back in and found one boy with his back pressed against the wall, whimpering. It sounded like the same whimper he'd heard just a moment ago.

"Hey," he said, keeping his voice soft and low. "If you don't want to go outside, you don't have to."

"I can't."

"It's okay. But it's really pretty out there."

"I'm afraid of heights. I don't want to fall like my mom did."

And what was Alex supposed to do with that information? These kids often had hard lives, often came from not just broken families but completely damaged backgrounds. It was part of the application process. They didn't just take boys who might need to get off the city streets, they took the ones that had major trauma in their lives, who'd lived through things no one should have to live through.

Now he could go two ways with this. He could leave him in here while he went out with the other kids. He'd be safe and Alex could listen for any commotion. He couldn't really leave seventeen kids outside on a railed porch forty feet above the ground. Or he could coax him out to see if he could replace a sad and terrible memory with something new.

"If I hold your hand, would that make it better? I promise it's beautiful. The sky is clear, and all the stars are up there just waiting to say hi to you."

Deep brown eyes searched his face, looking to see if he was lying. The little boy—Alex wished he knew his name—bit his lip.

Would he go for it? Alex tried hard to search his memory for how his dad might have handled this situation. But he'd been removed from so much of the day-to-day stuff that nothing came to him. So he waited and kept glancing outside to make sure no one got out of hand or truly did fall off the roof.

During one of his quick glances he felt a hand inch into his own. He didn't make a big deal out of it, and he didn't even look down. He just led the little boy out onto the observation deck and stood with seventeen other boys watching the night sky. A shooting star flew from the west to the east.

"Make a wish," he said to everyone and made one of his own.

****

The house was quiet, finally, with Manny tucked back under the covers. Liv leaned against the wall, watching his little chest rise and fall and wishing she could help him more. Her research had told her that night terrors were common and that the child didn't remember them when they did wake up. She hoped that really was true.

In the grips of the night terror, Manny had sat up in bed, eyes wide open, but he couldn't see her or hear her. She'd read it was best to not shake him or try to wake him up. It wasn't like a normal nightmare, but something more. So she rubbed his arm, spoke softly to him, and was thankful for the silence in which to do it. Davey and Uncle Bill had stayed, but the rest of the boys had cleared out.

She figured they were in the rec room, and she appreciated that. It kept them out of her hair and made it possible for her to quiet Manny down and get him back to sleep. Hopefully the rest of the night would be peaceful. Well, at least for everyone else. She had a feeling that now the crisis was over she was going to have to figure out what to do about that kiss she'd shared with Alex...

After putting Davey back to bed, she sent Bill off to his own room and then went hunting for the kids. She'd made it out to the hallway when she heard a mass of giggling, but not from the direction she had expected. Walking to the end of the hall, she looked up the stairs to find all of her boys, smiling and laughing as they made their way down the staircase almost no one used anymore.

And there was Alex behind them, also smiling and holding Freddy's hand. He bent down to hear something the quiet little first-timer said, shook his head, and then ruffled the boy's hair. They brought up the rear together. Every boy, from big to small, smiled at her as they walked past her, even the ones she hadn't been able to get to do more than just be politely silent. And somehow Alex had done this.

"Hey, Liv. Is Manny okay?" He paused in front of her. Freddy hugged him around the waist and then ran on quiet feet to catch up with the rest of the boys, who had turned into their rooms. No one made a sound except for the occasional creak of a bunk bed.

"He's fine. Do you mind if we talk downstairs? I don't want him to wake up."

"That's what I told the boys when we came in. They agreed to go stealth mode for the rest of the night." He quietly laughed at his own joke, and she had to stop herself from taking a step back or checking his forehead for fever.

Where had he gone with them, and what had happened? Leading the way to the kitchen, she ran through several different ways to start this conversation.

"Hot chocolate?" she asked as she went to the stove.

He took a seat at the island in the center of the kitchen with a smile on his handsome face. "Sure thing. I remember when Bill used to make hot chocolate in the winter. It was one of my favorite things to dip my toast in. Man, I haven't had that in years."

And the smile was still there. Every other time he'd talked about a memory or hedged around one, he'd frowned. It was as if they were painful, though she couldn't figure out why anything about being at Breathe would be painful. As though he didn't want to talk about anything having to do with this place, didn't want to have anything to do with this place. Until now.

"Toast this late at night might not be the best idea. But I can make a mean cup of cocoa."

"That would be great. Thanks. Is there anything I can do to help?'

The smile, the gratitude, and now an offer of help? Where did the thermometer go and how fast could she get it in his ear?

"Uh, no. I have this under control." She dipped down for a pan in the cupboard, keeping her back to him so he couldn't see her face. "So where did you take the boys?"

"Oh, just to an old hangout. Crockett used to take me up on the roof to look at the stars. I thought they might get a kick out of it."

She stood quickly and whipped around, almost losing her grip on the pan. "You took them onto the roof?"

"Yeah." He smiled. "They loved it. It has this great platform and a railing that runs the length of the thing. It was a widow's walk when the house was built. Crockett and I would go up there and stargaze in all seasons."

She honestly was speechless. As in, there were no words coming out of her mouth and she didn't know if she could have forced them from behind her teeth if her life depended on it. He'd taken them to the roof. *The roof!* One of them could have fallen off or been injured. She didn't even know there was a platform on the roof. She'd seen a structure of some sort, but Bill had told her it was useless and just for decoration. And Alex had taken her boys up there. "What were you *thinking*?"

Well, at least she'd found words, but from the way his smile dropped off his face, she had a feeling they hadn't been the right ones.

"What do you mean? It was perfectly safe. You needed them out of your hair so you could deal with Manny. I got them out of your hair. End of story."

"That is not the end of the story." She seethed for a moment. "That's three stories up, and dangerous. How sturdy is the railing? I bet that structure hasn't been touched in decades. Crockett never went up there when I was here. He didn't even mention the thing. And you just go trotting out with eighteen boys without a single thought to their safety." She banged the pot onto the stove and yanked ingredients for the hot chocolate out of the cabinet. At this point she might just put a dash of Tabasco sauce in there for good measure.

"I did think about their safety. I walked out and tested the platform and the railing myself. I made sure it was sound before anyone but me set a foot out there. They enjoyed themselves and were still smiling and quiet when they came back in. You got to do your job. What is your problem?"

"I don't have all night to talk about the problems in that, so let me just say that I do not want you to ever do that again. I cannot send home a kid that's fallen from three stories up with some excuse about a stargazing night."

He rose to his full height from the island, crossing his arms over his broad chest. "You might want to think about who you're talking to before you put your foot down. I'm not an idiot. I don't know what your deal is. Are you really mad that I took them out onto a safe platform, or are you mad that I was able to make them smile without your help?"

"How dare you!"

Bill rushed into the kitchen, his bathrobe flapping around his knees. "The boys can hear you upstairs. *I* can hear you upstairs without any trouble at all. What are you doing?"

Liv clamped her lips tightly together to keep herself from crying. So many emotions tumbled through her, from fear to anger to sadness, that she didn't know which to deal with first.

Alex eyed her from head to toe before answering Bill. "Liv and I were having a discussion about the platform on the roof. She feels it was dangerous to take the boys out."

Bill's eyes went from her to Alex and back to her. Alex had been far nicer about what she'd said than she had been in saying it. She'd told her boss what he could and couldn't do. If he'd been looking for an excuse to get rid of her or close the camp down, she'd just handed him the first piece wrapped in a bow.

"That platform is safe, Liv." Bill kept his disappointed gaze on her. "I've maintained it for years, ever since Alex left. Crockett wouldn't go up on it anymore, but I hoped that one day he would, so I kept it up, changing wood as necessary and making sure the thing remained sturdy."

And now she just wanted to cry. Just hide

somewhere and bawl her eyes out. "Why haven't you told me about it? You always said it was for decoration."

Bill glanced at Alex for a moment as if wondering if he should say what he wanted. Then he shrugged. "I was keeping it for the day when Alex came back, so he and his dad would still have that place they'd spent so much time. Even after Crockett left us too early, I hoped that one day Alex would be here."

She chanced a look at Alex and was struck by the hollow look in his eyes. She spoke to Bill, but her gaze remained on Crockett's son. "Thank you, Bill. I appreciate you taking care of it. Maybe now that Alex has been up there we can start using it in remembrance of Crockett. Alex and I should speak alone now. I promise to keep my voice down. Thanks for interrupting what could have gotten out of hand."

As Bill walked out of the kitchen, he clapped a hand on Alex's shoulder. "That man was devastated when you left. I know you think he chose this farm over his family, but he wasn't given a choice."

The hollow look on Alex's face went to downright haunted.

Alex turned to follow Bill, and she stopped him with a light hand on his forearm. "I'm sorry. I didn't know about the place, or Bill's upkeep, and I am sometimes overprotective of the boys. I want everyone to be safe. I thought they were just in the rec room. Finding out they'd been on the roof threw me off. I really am sorry."

"It's fine," he said, his voice dull, his gaze on the floor. "I'm glad Bill cleared things up. I'm going to head up to bed, unless you need anything else."

"Alex, look at me." When he did, she almost wished she hadn't asked him to. "It's going to be okay. I'm glad you took the boys up, and from their smiles, they loved it. Maybe we can move the telescope from the garage to the platform and do some real stargazing. I have a book of the constellations somewhere. Maybe you could show them to the boys. They'd love that. And I know they trust you."

"But do you trust me? Do you trust me, Liv? I've let this camp run for years without interfering because I trusted you. And yet ever since I've stepped foot on the property you've treated me like I don't belong. Like I've never belonged. And that's why my mother moved me away. And now I was just told my father didn't get a chance to choose to fight for me. I'm a little rough at the moment."

She'd seen this look before. When a kid didn't get any mail from their parents. When no one called to see how they were doing. When another week went by without knowing if they were even missed.

And she knew what her usual response was. So she used it now because he was hurting and deserved more than the hand he'd been given.

Stepping into him, she wrapped her arms around his waist. It wasn't like giving a kid a hug at all, but she'd just turn off the part of her brain that was noticing how masculine he was and how good he smelled and just hold on as a friend, as someone who was concerned for him and his well-being.

Alex stood with his arms stiff at his sides for the length of ten heartbeats, and then he crushed her to him.

They didn't say anything, both just breathing for the moment. She didn't know what to say and had no way of knowing what was running through his mind. The silence was not uncomfortable, but she wished she knew how to break it without making him hurt more.

He kissed the top of her head and stepped back. "I think I'll head to bed. We'll see what tomorrow brings."

She was left to wonder what that meant as she watched him walk away.

****

Alex lay in bed after leaving Liv and couldn't get to sleep. He'd done a ton of work today. More than he normally did, physically at least. He should be sleeping like a baby. Instead, he got up and paced for the third time in twenty minutes.

His father had not been given a choice.

Was that true? Or was it just the way Bill remembered it? What Crockett had told him when Alex's mother left never to return?

But was it true? He wouldn't ask his mother until he had more information. Part of him knew that she had only had his best interest in mind, but he hadn't been kidding when he'd told Liv he felt rough.

And that brought him to another question.

Had he been selfish? How had he not realized there was no way Liv had any kind of personal life throughout the entire summer?

To be honest, and he was being honest with himself, in the dark and where no one could judge him, he'd never even given it a thought. As far as he was concerned, Liv was here and doing what she loved. He got to stay out of this godforsaken place and still keep to the letter of his father's will. Every month she sent progress reports, and he emailed with her. She always sounded upbeat and happy to have this position that Crockett had groomed her for.

But at what cost?

Even if Crockett hadn't been given a choice, he still hadn't left the camp after his mother had packed Alex up and out of Breathe. So even if it wasn't intended, Crockett had chosen the camp over his family, and now Liv chose the camp too. Was her son happy here? Why did he sleep with the other campers when he must have his own bed? Did he feel like she loved the campers more than him?

He thought about that for a few seconds, running over his interactions with the boy even when he hadn't known he belonged to Liv. He seemed happy, but then so had Alex even when he sought out Becky at the Dish to console him after yet another fight between his parents.

And what would Liv have done tonight if Alex hadn't been here? She had needed room and silence to work with the poor screaming kid. Alex respected Bill, but the man was getting older. She had the whole thing on her shoulders. All of it.

It was stupid in the extreme. He would have to think about hiring another person, someone who could work directly under Liv but would give her a break every once in a while. A camp host, maybe.

It was a brilliant idea, and he sat up most of the night diagramming how it would work and how to let Liv know. She might not like it at first, but she would see the reason behind it once he explained it to her.

With that in mind, he finally got some sleep and woke to the smells of Bill's cooking directly below him. He hadn't eaten this well in years. This was something he could get used to, he thought as he dressed in another borrowed outfit. This one had no initials on it, and he felt better.

Tromping down the stairs, he made a beeline for the dining room, where everyone was chattering excitedly over omelets and fried potatoes. Bill had also laid out platters of fruit every few seats, and those were surprisingly being eaten too.

Then again, he saw Bill's assistant walk up and down behind the kids' seats and push the fruit on them if they hadn't taken any already. Smart lady.

All in all, he had to say this Breathe was much better run than the one his father had inherited all those years ago. There were no fights breaking out at the table. No one wore gang colors or bandanas or threw gang signs. Not that things had been terrible when Crockett had been the owner, he just hadn't had this much control, to the detriment of Alex and his whole family unit.

Liv walked in, breaking his train of thought. He was all too happy to forget those memories and think about the way she moved across the floor, waving to everyone and exchanging a few words with each of the kids. She really paid attention to everyone and knew each of their names. From the way Bill had talked earlier, there were quite a few returning kids, but there were also new ones. And he couldn't help but admire the way they each seemed to look up to her and respect her.

When she came close to his spot at the table, he reached out and tugged the ponytail brushing below her shoulder blades.

"Aren't you going to say good morning to me?"

She peered at him for moment, probably trying to read him after their exchange last night. He was just going to ignore the whole thing for the moment and think about it back in the comfort of his townhouse. Too many years had passed for anything to change at this point.

"Of course," she said. "I was just on my way to get some food before these growing boys eat it all. I'll be right back."

The words were right, but she avoided his eyes the entire time. Would she now want to avoid him, after he almost broke last night?

He'd just have to find out.

Chapter Eight

The bacon smelled heavenly and the omelets were exactly to her liking. Green peppers and melty cheese made her mouth water. She scooped some fried potatoes onto her plate and thanked heaven that Betty hadn't made them or they would have been five-alarm hot.

And she would have to face Alex at some point, so there was no point in continuing to procrastinate over which drink she wanted, since she always drank orange juice.

Making her way back over to the table, she chose the one seat that was available. The one right next to Alex.

"So did you end up getting some sleep last night?" she asked before he could say anything. She was determined to take control of the conversation and not let it go anywhere she wasn't comfortable. There was something about last night, and the way they had sat together at the small wire table, that had been too intimate, too comfortable for her own good. And then the way he'd kissed her and the way the night ended. Too many emotions, too many things to process for her to know how to act.

"I finally did, once I got some of that sugar through my system." His smile crinkled the corners of his eyes. "Remind me not to eat so much so late at night."

As if she'd ever be in that position again.

But she said, "Will do," and dug into her breakfast, ready to get this day started and get her mind as far away from last night and the feelings she'd experienced as possible.

After finishing off her omelet and part of her fried potatoes, she had eaten more than she probably should have. But then Marcy came by on her fruit patrol.

"I hope you're going to at least eat some of the cantaloupe your uncle cut up this morning. You have to set a good example for the boys, after all."

Nothing like a little guilt to make the melon go down.

But Liv took some, as Alex watched with an amused smile on his face.

"Good?"

"Yes," she mumbled.

"You know, you are the director and can tell her you aren't hungry. Hell, you're an adult and could tell her the same thing."

"Watch the language. We don't tolerate that here."

"Oh, right, sorry."

"Just don't do it again."

"Aye, aye, captain."

She had sounded downright grumpy, and she shouldn't be. The sun was shining, the birds were tweeting outside the open windows, and a fabulous breeze was rippling the curtains in the dining room. There was nothing to be sullen about. Except for the fact that last night all she had done was dream the end of her evening with Alex over and over again, but this time with him kissing her on the mouth again instead of walking away looking like his world had crashed.

She stood up too quickly and was nearly out the door before she heard Alex call out behind her, "Hey, if you have time today, I'd like to go over a couple things with you."

"Sure, I'll make time after I get back from my meeting."

"Do you need any help? Anything I can do for the meeting, or is it a secret girl thing?"

As if. "I have the meeting under control, but thanks. Why don't you see what the boys are doing today and help out there?"

He gave her the raised eyebrow and she ignored it this time. She had things to do, anything to do that would get her away from him for just a little while to regain her equilibrium.

An hour later, the inside of Petri's Dish was bustling on Wednesday morning, and she was working overtime to not pull out her hair. Liv held court at the table in the back, trying to persuade all the lovely older women that they truly did want to help out just one more time with fundraising. In these economic times, it was even more important to provide a safe place for kids to spend some time in the summer where they could see that there was so much more to offer than gangs and street violence.

"Mathilda, I just need you to see about finishing up the details of the cook-off. You're so wonderful at organizing everything that I can't imagine this is more than you can handle, especially with everyone here helping you."

Mathilda preened for a moment, until Karen Myers made a sour face at her.

"I don't think Mathilda is qualified, quite honestly.

I bet she thinks this is too much for her and she just doesn't want to say it." Karen crossed her arms over her enormous bosom with a smug smile on her face.

If Liv didn't step in soon, they might come to blows across their sticky buns and coffee. "Ladies, you both have your strengths. Now, Karen, I know that Mathilda has been absolutely instrumental in so many things that have to do with Breathe and with raising money to help out all these wonderful kids who just need a chance. And you are so excellent at making sure all the food and drinks are up to snuff. I know you can do that with your hands tied behind your back. I'm counting on you."

Nodding her agreement, Karen still had her arms crossed, but her face was softer around the mouth. If Liv never had to talk another person into doing something they just should do because it was the right thing, she would be in heaven. Maybe she should have allowed Alex to come along. He could have buttered them up for her. But that wasn't going to happen anytime soon, so she might as well buck it up and get the rest of the roster full.

"So can I count on you, Mathilda? Now that Karen will be checking the food, I bet you're ready to take on the business of decorating the venue."

The two women had been rivals since high school, and Liv was not ashamed at all to use that mercilessly to get what she wanted, if she had to.

Mathilda nodded, looking like an exact replica of Karen. Liv held in a snicker. They always ended up agreeing, so she didn't know why they fought it. Putting a check mark next to both of their names, she moved on to the entertainment they'd advertised.

Or at least she tried to, except suddenly there was a commotion going on at the front of the diner, and everyone had stopped to stare.

Someone was hacking away—choking, really—at the front lunch counter. Liv jumped out of her seat before anyone else could rise and was through the swinging door from the back dining room before another cough came. Using her first-aid training, she locked her arms around a man's torso and nearly lifted him off the stool while giving him the Heimlich maneuver. She waited to hear that telltale swift inhale that meant whatever was lodged in the man's throat had come out.

But the sound never came and she started to panic. And in her panic she worked harder. "Is he turning blue?" she asked as she used her fisted hands to apply more pressure.

"You're going to kill him," Betty said, draping a towel over her shoulder. "He's not choking, hon. He just had a taste of my hash browns with my special chili pepper sauce and probably wants a glass a water, not the life forced out of him."

Liv dropped her hands from around the guy's very firm middle and stepped back, her face flaming as she wished she could just drop through a hole, any hole, in the floor. She really hoped she hadn't hurt him.

She wanted to run, but she had been taught better than that. "I'm sorry," she mumbled as she watched Alex make a grab for a tall, sweating glass of water in front of him and gulp it all down in a long series of swallows that did incredible things to the column of his throat.

"It's okay," he croaked once Betty put another

glass of water at his elbow. "If I ever am really choking, I'd want you there."

She didn't think it was possible, but her face flamed even harder. She had to be the color of a fire hydrant, and all she wanted to do was escape, so she did. Her table in the back was abuzz with her unneeded heroics, and any further promises and details would have to wait until later, when she started making phone calls to rally the troops. All the women had gotten a good look at the familiar handsome man, and speculation was rife on whose daughter would be best for him and how long he was going to be in the area. They each wanted Alex for someone else.

The women started wandering away long before Liv was done, but she had lost control when she'd taken off to do her over-achiever Good Samaritan thing. And as always, it seemed to bite her in the butt.

She waved to the last of the four women who had been at the table before she ran off. Watching them walk out the door, she shook her head because the boys were waiting back at the farm, and she had wanted all this taken care of before now. But with everything going on, it had been her first chance to sit down with everyone. And now all she had were vague promises and an old rivalry holding the whole thing together when it was less than a week away.

Collecting her notebook and folders from the old-style diner table, Liv took longer than absolutely necessary, hoping the front of the place would be mostly cleared out before she showed her face again. She wished she could sneak out the back, but that would mean going through the kitchen. And she really didn't want to come face to face with Betty after she'd assaulted one of her customers.

Stacking all the plates in the middle of the table, she then dumped the contents of all the glasses into one glass so that cleanup would be easier. Silverware went into another cup, with the handles facing up. She spent several minutes avoiding the people out front by doing the busywork she'd done in her teenage years when she'd been a busgirl here. But there was only so much she could do. It wasn't going to get any easier if she took too long.

She'd just have to put her brave face on and march out like she had known what she was doing. Hopefully Alex wouldn't mention it, and she wouldn't think about how good he had felt under her hands.

She tried that and ended up scurrying out the door without a single word to anyone. She had an account with the diner, so she didn't have to pay the tab, plus she'd remembered to leave a tip large enough to cover everyone. A couple of people called out goodbyes as she left and she lifted a hand in answer while ducking out the door. She was nearly clear, by her car and ready to open the door, when she heard feet striking the sidewalk with purpose.

Where was a hole when you needed one? Seriously. She wanted to fall right in and not come back out for, say, ten or twelve years. If he'd thought of her before now as a Good Samaritan type, your typical girl next door, or a goody two shoes, that was certainly reinforced when she leapt tall tables to get to someone who didn't even need to be saved. She should have her head checked.

The heavy weight of his hand settled on her shoulder. She stopped under the gentle pressure. Her cheeks burned with another blush, but she wouldn't be able to avoid him forever.

"So what did you have all those biddies in there for?" Alex asked.

Turning, she looked to see if he was laughing at her. He would mention her impromptu and unnecessary Heimlich at any minute, and then she'd have to smack him. But in the meantime he looked like he was serious.

"I'm planning the annual fundraiser with them."

"Yeah? Are you sure you want Mathilda and Karen working on anything together? I remember them being interfering pains in the ass when I was little. My dad stayed as far away from them as possible."

He remembered that? Interesting that he would even talk about it, since he hadn't wanted to talk about anything having to do with the past since he'd been here. Maybe he'd worked through some things overnight after Bill had hit him with information he didn't appear to have known before now.

And heck, if it saved her from having to talk about how she'd nearly killed him, then she was game.

"Actually, I think your dad just never approached them right. If you pit them against each other, then you're golden."

His chuckle was deep and rode the back of her neck. Now was not the time to start realizing that Alex was a whole lot more attractive than she'd let herself think. He had a rugged masculinity that she had never associated with city types.

"I'll have to use that when I get back to DC."

"And when is that going to be?"

His smile dimmed a little bit, but he put it right back into place. "Ready to get rid of me already? I just got here."

"But you're never here."

"Well, you've never needed me before."

"And I don't need you now." That hadn't come out quite the way she had meant it to, and his face went stony.

"Regardless, as I said, I'd like to stay for a few days and see in action how things run around here. I won't get in your way or cramp your style, Liv. I promise."

And what could have been a fun conversation, and a way for her to possibly get him more involved in what his father had loved, had just turned into him leaving angry. She was going to have to come up with a way to make it up to him. She hated that.

****

Back at the farm, Alex walked around the yard, working out his agitation. He seemed to never know how to say the right thing to Liv. And no matter how he tried to put memories of his father out of his head, he was everywhere. What had really happened when his mom decided to leave?

He'd gone to ask Betty for some advice and had ended up choking on his hash browns. Right before Liv had tried to kill him with the best intentions.

He chuckled softly before he also recalled that she'd told him she didn't need him.

That shut down the laugh altogether. Did she want him gone? Did he want to be gone? He wasn't sure which made his mood that much worse. He was used to being sure of himself, knowing his next step, having a very defined path. Yet here it was as if the whole world was turned upside down. He was enjoying kids and making memories. Enjoying the fresh air and actually falling asleep without sirens in the background. He hadn't ordered any fancy restaurant food since he'd been here, and he'd walked more over the last few days than he had in the last six months.

And he was good. For the most part. Physically, anyway.

This emotional stuff was for the birds, though. He hadn't thought about Breathe or his father in the last five years. Even before that it was only a passing thought if his father called.

Rounding the corner of the barn, he kicked a stone. Should he just leave now? He'd done his part. The farm was safe. Breathe was safe. The charges were dropped, and no one was getting into trouble. It did still rub him the wrong way that the real culprits hadn't been caught, but that wasn't what he'd been brought here for.

He could be home before the sun set, back in his townhouse, watching his large, flat-screen TV and enjoying a glass of wine. Meetings could be moved up from next week and his schedule could be full within ten minutes, if he called now.

He kicked another stone. What to do? His journey around the grounds took him to the next corner of the barn, the back wall that faced a pasture.

And there he found Liv's boy sneaking into the far door. Alex knew he was sneaking because the child glanced around and then opened the door only enough to squeeze through the opening. What was he up to?

It was none of Alex's business, but it could be if the kid was doing something he shouldn't be.

After taking about one second to think it over, Alex followed the boy. He had to know what was going on.

He'd deal with whatever it was once he knew the situation.

Opening the door only enough to squeeze through himself, Alex waited a moment for his eyes to adjust to the dim interior of the cavernous barn.

What was Davey up to? Was it something Alex would have to address with Liv? That was the last thing he wanted to do.

A soft chuffing sound came from a stall in a dark corner to his far right. A flashlight popped on, and Alex caught sight of a furry head and a long neck above a stall door. He'd never kept track of the animals they had on the premises, but he was pretty sure alpacas were not included with the horses and cows they typically kept.

Taking his time, Alex crept to the stall and kept just out of sight as he peeked over the wooden door. And there was Davey sitting on the straw-covered floor, his flashlight pointed at a picture book that he read to the two curious alpacas.

Thirty seconds in, Alex considered inching backwards and leaving the kid to his farm friends. He seemed contented and wasn't hurting anyone. The one alpaca had curled itself up next to Davey and rested its head on his shoulder, appearing to actually look at the pictures.

But then Alex remembered the two missing alpacas from the Beckham farm. And the fact that he would have had to sign off on buying alpacas for Breathe. As far as he could remember, he'd never done that. He probably would have said no, since his father had been against the things when he was younger.

So were these the same animals? The ones missing

from Beckham's farm? How had they gotten here? And what was he supposed to do now that he'd found them and Liv's kid?

The thought of inching away, not to leave them alone but to get Liv, took on a new urgency. Alex did not want to be responsible for Beckham's animals being on Breathe's property. They'd just gotten back into the man's good graces after starting the process of fixing the damage next door. How would they explain his animals being here in their barn? And why were they in the barn? How had they gotten here?

Taking a step back, his foot landed on a pitchfork that came up and whapped him in the rear end. Not exactly the funny slapstick from old TV shows when it happened to you. He couldn't help the groan that came out of his mouth, which of course alerted Davey to the fact that he wasn't alone.

The flashlight blinked out at the same time Alex heard a small whimper in the dark.

After a full minute had passed with no other sound, Alex admitted that someone was going to have to break the silence. Since he was the adult, it should be him.

"Look, I know you're in here. I can't leave until I find out what happened. I'm not going to tell on you, but I do need to know how the animals got here."

There was that whimper again. Alex wished he had his own flashlight. Was the kid afraid of the dark? Afraid of him? Afraid of getting in trouble? Had he been the one to set the alpacas free? If he had, then that could mean that other boys from the camp had been with him and had in fact done the vandalism that they swore they hadn't done.

Yet they'd had alpacas for a few days, at this point,

and no one had known. What were the chances they weren't related? Nil. Damn.

"I can't."

"Turn the flashlight on, Davey, and we'll talk about this. I can't leave until I talk to you. And I don't want to do that in the dark."

The flashlight popped back on. Alex was taken aback at the sadness in the boy's eyes.

"You're gonna tell my mom, and she's going to yell."

Alex shrugged, not knowing what else to do. Of course he couldn't keep this from Liv, but, man, how he wished he could. He remembered the very few times Crockett had been disappointed in him. It had crushed him.

"First, let's talk about how they got here, and then we'll talk about what to do about it."

"I didn't steal them." Davey petted the one next to him. The other one obviously wanted in on the action because it lay down on his other side and nudged his hand.

"I'm not saying you did, but they're here and they shouldn't be. Mr. Beckham has been looking for them for days. How long have you known they were here?"

"Since I put them here," Davey whispered.

Resisting the urge to smack his own forehead, Alex leaned against the wall. This was going to be complicated no matter how he spun it, and he was pretty good at spinning.

"And when was that?"

"The night some kids spray painted the barn and broke the fence."

Oh, man. Did that mean Davey had been there?

Had Alex given that pep talk and gotten all those smiles for nothing? "And how did you get them to follow you?"

"I go over there to play with them sometimes, so when they saw me, they galloped over looking for blackberries."

"And where did you see you?"

"Outside their fence." His head dropped into the neck of the alpaca to the right, and his shoulders shook.

Jesus, was he crying? He couldn't do this. "Hey, Davey, nothing that we can't fix. Don't cry, please."

The boy turned his head and laid it against the alpaca. He looked broken, more broken than an eight-year-old should be. "You have to tell Mom?"

"I'm sorry, but I do. We can't keep Beckham's animals."

"But he doesn't want them anymore! He said he was going to sell them. When I asked Mom if we could buy them, she said that you'd never let us buy them so I'd better stop asking. I told her I'd buy them with my own money, but she just shook her head."

Alex didn't know what to say to that. Fortunately, the kid was still talking, so Alex let him continue his rant.

"So I went over to say goodbye to them, and there were boys over at the farm and they were doing bad things. The fence was already broken, I don't know how they did it, but Murray and Alfred were still in there."

Was he talking about the alpacas or the boys? Alex couldn't recall anyone with either of those names.

Davey patted his furry friends. "Murray came first, and then Alfred. I already had the blackberry branches because I wanted to say goodbye in a good way, but then when they came to me through the broken fence, I ran and they followed."

"And they ended up in here because you don't want Mr. Beckham to sell them to anyone else."

"Yeah," Davey said quietly, wiping his nose on his shirt. "I'll go tell Mom. At least I got to spend some time with them before they left."

The kid was breaking his heart. Brave and willing to tell on himself? If Alex had any doubt Liv was taking care of her son and raising him well, that laid it to rest immediately.

"Can we talk for a minute about these boys you said you saw?"

Davey shook his head and slapped a hand over his mouth. The alpaca that'd lost his petting butted at Davey.

"Just tell me if they were from the camp."

Shaking his head, Davey kept his hand over his mouth.

Give him a recalcitrant executive any time, not a kid. And then Alex recalled one of Crockett's most prized tactics. "Okay, let's deal. I'll give your mom the pass to buy the alpacas if you tell me who you saw."

Chapter Nine

"You're going to bribe me?"

Davey's words surprised a laugh out of Alex. "Ever heard the expression 'you shouldn't look a gift horse in the mouth'?"

"No."

"It means don't question it when it comes to getting what you want."

"But I can't tell." The boy dug his fingers into the animal's fur, his face obviously scared. Part of Alex didn't want to push, but the other part wanted the names of the kids. Breathe and the kids who found refuge here for the summer should not have to carry the burden of a crime they didn't commit.

"I need the names, Davey. Don't you want to make sure that the right people get punished?"

"I don't want anyone to be punished."

"But the boys here, your friends, have been punished, and it's not right."

"I'll get in trouble, though. I don't get to leave at the end of the summer, and then it'll just be me and them, and they'll know I told."

Now they were getting somewhere. It had been kids who lived here, not the campers. And didn't Alex feel like a loser for not even believing, at first, that was possible? After being with them over the last several days, though, he knew there was no way the boys at

113

Breathe would have defaced Beckham's property. But without names there was nothing he could do. He had to have names.

"I'll handle it. I promise your name will not be mentioned. I don't want them going around and hurting anything or anyone else. I have to know who you saw."

"You promise? And then I can have my friends?" Davey asked in a small voice.

"I promise. And I'll talk to your mom about the friends."

"What are you promising and what friends?" Liv said from the doorway.

She stalked closer, and Alex mentally ran through a series of ways to handle this. He'd wanted to do it on his own time, in a sequence that would get him the best results. But it looked like he was going to have to wing it. Especially when she stalked closer.

"What is going on?" Standing on tiptoe, she tried to peek over Alex's shoulder.

He bobbed and weaved as necessary to keep her looking right at him. "I need to speak with you outside."

"No, I need to know what is going on."

He drew himself to his full height. "As the owner of Breathe, I need to speak with the director of Breathe—outside, right now. Please come with me." He used his hard boardroom voice, the one he had to pull out when he was trying to help someone and they refused to listen.

The frustration and the worry on her face were almost enough to have him backing down. Almost. Instead he put his hand under her elbow and escorted her back out the way she'd come in. The whole time, she continued to glance back over her shoulder. Fortunately Davey had turned the flashlight off, so there was nothing to see in the dim interior.

She shook him off two steps out of the door. When he closed the door behind him and then leaned back against it, she faced him down like an angry mama bear.

"How dare you! What the hell do you think you're doing?"

"Language." The word was out of his mouth before he thought how that was just going to fuel her rage.

"Don't play games with me on my own turf, or you will lose. Now tell me what in the world is going on, or I'll show you exactly what happens to people who stand between me and my son." Furious was an understatement. He had no doubt she could probably pile-drive him into the ground with just a look at this point. But there was more at stake here, if he could just get her to listen. But how?

"Give me two minutes." She snorted, and he continued anyway. "Two minutes. Davey is safe. I promise."

"You're making a lot of promises lately, it seems."

"Two minutes," he said with steel in his voice.

"Fine. Two minutes. And it better be good, or boss or not, it will not be pretty."

He had no doubt.

"Can we go to your cottage?" As soon as he asked he knew he shouldn't have.

"Here or nowhere, and this is eating into your two minutes."

"Here it is, then." Sticking his hands into his pockets, he rocked back on his heels, keeping his back to the door. "Davey saw the boys who did the vandalism. He doesn't want to say who because he doesn't want to get into trouble. He said that he doesn't get to go home after summer like everyone else here, which leads me to believe that the culprits are from Langstown. I promised him that if he told me who they are I would keep his name out of it."

She chewed on that for about fifteen seconds. "Why wouldn't you let me look at Davey? Does he have a black eye? Did someone hit him because he wouldn't tell?"

His gut clenched. He'd had tussles with the kids in town when he was younger and almost lost a tooth when he was punched in the face for defending one of their campers. It was shortly before his mom took off with him to—in her words—a better environment. Had that been the final straw?

"Has that happened before?"

"Once, and it will never happen again. You didn't answer my question, and your two minutes are almost up."

"Didn't you hear the part about Davey knowing who did this?"

"I did, and believe me when I say I want to know as bad as you do, if not more, but first I need to make sure my son is okay."

"Your son is fine. There is a slight issue, though, that I'd like to discuss with you before we go back in."

She arched her eyebrows at him and crossed her arms.

"It seems he picked up a few strays at the Beckhams' place when he saw the kids. Murray and Alfred."

Now she was the one rocking back on her heels. "He stole the two alpacas and didn't tell anyone, not even when Beckham demanded the return of his animals?" She massaged her forehead. "It's all going to fall to pieces. It won't matter that the boys here didn't vandalize the barn, especially when my own child stole alpacas."

"He didn't steal them. They followed him after the fence was broken by the vandals." Hedging around the truth was not something Alex liked to do, but this was a time of necessity.

"And what was he doing over there in the first place?" She blew out a breath. "Why am I even asking you? Your two minutes are up. Now get out of my way so I can see my kid."

"One more thing."

The sound that came out of her mouth was less groan and more growl.

"I promised Davey he could keep the alpacas, which I will pay for, if he tells us who the kids are."

"Bribery?" she nearly yelled.

"Hey, it was Crockett's best tool, he always used to say. Being that he's your idol, I would have thought you'd approve."

"Get out of my way. That is the wrong thing to finally pick up from your dad."

"I can't move until you promise me something."

She faced off with him, and totally inappropriate thoughts zinged through his head when he should have been concerned about the confrontation. This woman was strong, opinionated, and tough. She was also beautiful and intelligent. If he ever truly considered settling down, she would be his ideal woman, as long as

117

she lived in the city. But she didn't, and she was furious, and he'd better get moving before she moved him.

"For God's sake, spit it out so I can tell you 'no' and we can move on." She was less than a half step from him. The scent of her perfume tickled his nose.

He breathed in. "Don't be mad at him. He's trying really hard. It's difficult to love something but not be able to keep it. He loves those alpacas, and he was willing to come tell you himself this afternoon. He actually said that at least he got to spend some time with them before yet one more thing leaves him behind." Alex paused for a moment. Had the kid actually said that or was Alex speaking for himself from years ago?

"He's never left behind."

"But isn't he? Every year you bring in all these kids, and they go back to their lives but he stays and has to make friends with kids who don't spend the summer with him. They go on vacations with their parents and go to the beach, and he's here. Always here."

Her arms relaxed from the way they'd been clenched around her waist. "Are you sure we're still talking about Davey?"

"Of course." But he wasn't sure. Davey hadn't said any of those things. In fact the kid had looked happy every time he'd seen him, and he got to really be in the thick of things, unlike Alex when he was that age. He could just love the alpacas and not worry about being left behind, because he knew the people here loved him.

"I'm going in to see my son." She took that half step and was a breath away from being flush up against his chest.

It was stunning how much he wanted her to lean into him.

"I'd like you to let him keep the alpacas."

"And have him think it's not only okay to steal but also to be bribed?"

Her scent engulfed him at this distance. "Yes. It's not as if he'll truly think that. He knows he did the wrong thing, and he was going to tell you. You have to believe that."

She rubbed her forehead. He wanted to capture her hand and bring it to his lips. That desire had him wanting to back up. If he'd had room, he would have.

"I'll have to think about it. But first, I want those names and I want this settled. Now move." She looked up at him with something in her eyes that he couldn't define. "Please."

And so he moved, not sure if he'd just won or lost a lot more than he had bargained for when he'd driven out to this place that held so many memories and so many crushed dreams.

****

"Davey?" Liv stepped back from Alex as her child came around the side of the barn. She still hadn't decided how she'd handle this and had hoped for a moment alone while looking for the boy. A moment out of the presence of Alex and his eyes, his hands, his scent that seemed to surround her. Her head was going in so many directions. She'd just wanted a minute of quiet, but she wasn't going to get it now.

Davey walked the few remaining steps to them and stood next to Alex.

Putting her hands on her hips, she frowned at her son, her heart, and wondered what on earth she was going to do with this boy who meant more than anything to her. Was she cheating him out of a better life by keeping him out here? Making him interact with kids who had much harsher lives than he would ever experience, she hoped? To her it had been a saving grace to be brought here, but he'd always been here and didn't know anything else.

"I'm sorry, Mom. I went over to say goodbye to Murray and Alfred with their favorite treat, and the fence was broken, and I knew they were going to be sold, and I wanted them so bad, and then they followed me, and I just couldn't send them back." He pressed himself flat against the door, his fingers curling into the wood. Alex stood next to him, offering nothing.

"Davey, this is not a good thing. Mr. Beckham has been looking for these guys for days. Why didn't you tell me they were here? I could have returned them the first day." And she would have known who had done the damage to her neighbor's property. Would have been able to save herself from calling Alex up here and putting herself into a tailspin over a man she'd had so little to do with over the last fifteen years.

"I'm sorry." A single tear leaked out of her son's eye, and he sniffed. Using his fist, he swiped the tear away, then bit his lip. "You're going to have to punish me, and I'll go explain myself to Mr. Beckham. I know I shouldn't have done this. It's bad. I'm bad. I'm sorry. I just was afraid those boys would hurt Murray and Alfred, and I wasn't thinking. I'm sorry, Mom."

Getting on her knees in the dirt, she hugged Davey to her. "Baby, you're not bad. I wish I would have known sooner or known how important these guys were to you."

"I didn't want to bother you more, because camp was starting. I know how busy you get trying to do all the things you do. I stay out of your way as much as I can."

God, was that what he thought she wanted? She didn't even chance a look at Alex. She didn't want to see his face. "I always want you in my way. And no matter how busy I get, I always have time for you. Always."

She hugged him to her again, and he buried his face in her shoulder. Alex still hadn't said anything. She couldn't help but glance up at him, and when she did, she couldn't read his expression. It appeared to be part hope, part sadness. But why?

That was a concern for another time. Now she needed to deal with the mess her big-hearted child had created. She took Davey's precious face into her hands. "Let's get cleaned up. You and I are going to go over to Mr. Beckham and let him know that you've had the alpacas. I don't know how he's going to take that, but we have to be honest. No lies, remember? Then we'll see what happens from there." She was going to take her personal checkbook with her and buy these two. Davey would take care of them all by himself. He was old enough to clean up after them, to make sure they had food and water and got a chance to run around outside. Alex was obviously okay with them being here.

Alex. Being near him made her heart flutter for about the hundredth time, and she alternately wished he'd go as quickly as possible and stay forever.

Looking at Alex again, she found him with his hands deep in his pockets, his arms stiff, and his face grim. Was he getting ready to take her on again? Talk her into letting Davey have the animals? Defend her son's actions? Tell her how Crockett would have handled this?

Curiosity had her wanting to see what he had to say, and self-preservation had her just wanting to get things over with so he could go home.

"And what are you going to tell Beckham?" he asked her.

"I'll talk to him," Davey answered. "I'm the one who did it and should stand up and apologize when I do wrong."

Davey sounded so happy saying it, but when it came out like that it made her feel she was being too harsh. The grim look on Alex's face turned downright frosty. "You're going to make him stand up to the man by himself? He didn't hurt anyone. We can return the animals if the old guy wants them. Are you just going to send him in and wait out on the porch while he takes his licks?"

"What is wrong with you?" she demanded. "Of course not. I'm not sending him into some kind of firing squad. I'm going to go with him, but we can't lie, and this has to be taken care of."

"He's your kid." He shrugged.

"You are absolutely right."

Davey's gaze bounced back and forth between them during the exchange. Was she doing the wrong thing? But what else could she do?

"He is my kid, and I will take care of him and this. Why don't you just go home? I ran this whole operation without you just fine. You can sign the checks, I'll send you emails, and we'll go back to how it was before."

Taking Davey's hand, she walked away, absolutely

fuming. Who did he think he was? As if she didn't have her child's best interest at heart and know what was best. Of course she'd never dealt with a situation like this before, but they'd get through it.

Davey pulled her to stop when he didn't come along with her.

"What's wrong?" she asked.

"I want Alex to go with us."

"Honey, I can handle this. Alex doesn't need to go with us." She ignored the fact that they were talking about him as if he weren't standing right there. "It really is going to be okay. You took care of the alpacas. I'm sure they're in good health, and we'll just explain to Mr. Beckham that you were afraid they were going to get hurt by the boys. Can you tell me who they were?"

Glancing down at Davey, she could only groan to herself when he shook his head. Being able to give Mr. Beckham names of the true troublemakers would go a long way toward putting this all behind them.

"Please, Davey. It's important."

"Uh-uh. I'm only going to tell Alex. He promised he'd protect me. I trust him."

Now she groaned out loud. "Davey, I'm your mom. I'll protect you, but I need those names."

"Alex only." To demonstrate his point, he pulled his hand out of hers and gripped Alex's tightly.

To his credit the man didn't pull away, though his whole face registered surprise.

So what would he do now?

"Better go get changed," she said to her boss, wanting to see Alex in action and what he would do when pushed. If he'd thought she was going to leave

Davey to fend for himself, then he could see firsthand how wrong he'd been. And if it got the names of the true vandals, then she had no problem dragging Alex along with them to explain the alpaca debacle.

Chapter Ten

Alex had learned his lesson and dressed more appropriately to visit the Beckham Farm this time. Bill gave him another pair of jeans and a shirt, assuring him they had plenty. Apparently, Liv picked up clothes from the local Ladies' Auxiliary thrift store in case any child came without enough. Between those clothes and what had been able to be re-used from Crockett's wardrobe after his death, Alex was covered for as long as he was here.

After Bill found him something suitable, Alex used the time in his room to place a quick call to Mr. Beckham to warn him they were coming over about the alpacas.

He could have considered that dishonest and against what Liv wanted him to do, but since he hadn't asked her, he did it with a clear conscience. Well, a semi-clear conscience. That was good enough for him.

"I have a favor to ask," he said when Beckham finally got to the phone.

"Boy, there's not much I wouldn't have done for your father, but I don't know what I can do for you."

He outlined what had happened with the alpacas. Beckham blustered at first, and that was what Alex had figured the man would do. Alex was willing to take the tongue-lashing for the boy, though. As long as it got him what he wanted in the end.

"I understand you're not happy, but I have to tell you this boy is something else. He is willing to come tell you himself and apologize. He expects to be told he's bad for doing it and that he should be punished. And he's not even angry about it. He's ready to take whatever punishment you think he should have because he's happy he at least got to spend some time with the alpacas before you sold them to the highest bidder."

Beckham harrumphed. Alex had heard that sound before from clients who had been resistant to making any changes until Alex laid it all out for them with pie charts and graphs and solid projections. It was the sound of being impressed but not wanting to commit to anything yet.

Alex just had to seal the deal and this could be finished. He'd keep his promise to Davey, make Liv happy, and give those names to Beckham so he could press charges against the right people. Especially since there wasn't a lot left to do for them to work it off with their own sweat and blood. His boys had already done most of it.

His boys…

"You bring that boy over here, and I'll make him a deal. It'll be like the old days with your dad when you got caught doing something you shouldn't." Beckham laughed. "Those were good times. So let's just forget we had this conversation and let him say his piece. I'll act suitably impressed, and then we'll shake on a price for those wooly beasts. The wife wanted them, but I don't have the patience for them. I grow corn, for God's sake."

Alex chuckled.

"Damn things made noise all the time and were

more like pets. It'll be good for them to go to someone who'll care for them."

"Davey will do a good job. He already has been." Alex cleared his throat. "The other matter is a little touchier."

"Go ahead, boy. Spit it out."

"It seems Davey saw the boys who did the damage to your place, but he doesn't want to tell us their names because he has to go school with them at the end of the summer."

Beckham blew out a breath on the other side of the line. "I was afraid of that. Look, the damage is fixed, pretty much, and I appreciate your boys doing the hard work. I don't think much is going to come from turning them in. I want them punished, though, and I'll talk to their fathers individually. Let's not go further than that."

Alex knew when to back off to make a deal possible and when to compromise. He was willing to keep his mouth shut for the moment, but once he heard those names, he might be the one talking to fathers instead of leaving that to Beckham. First, they had to get the alpacas and go through the motions of letting Davey be a responsible eight-year-old.

"We'll be over in fifteen minutes."

"I'll have the missus make some sweet tea since I didn't give you a chance to drink yours last time."

"Great." Alex groaned when he pushed the off circle on his phone. He pulled on a polo shirt and a fresh pair of jeans. He was zippering up when a knock sounded on his door.

Opening it, he expected to see Liv. Instead he found himself staring at Bill. The older man took him in from head to toe.

"Well, at least you're dressed right this time."

"You're the one who gave me the clothes, old man." Alex chuckled at the picture he must have made going to see the farmer in his tie and pressed slacks. "Yes, I think this time might go better than last time."

"Last time didn't go so badly, Alex. Don't underestimate what you did. You didn't know the boys here, so you just did the best you could with what you had."

"I should have given them more credit. I should have listened before I assumed I knew what had happened."

Bill smiled at him, and Alex felt like he'd just brought home the highest score on a test in junior high. Back in the day, when he made good grades, Bill would make him a cake and list all his grades on it in icing. He hadn't thought about that in years.

"Anyway, hopefully we can put this all to bed now."

Bill chuckled. "The boy really had those alpacas in the barn for the last five days?"

"Yeah, smart little thing, to keep them in the back so no one knew."

"He is smart. Smart as you were."

"Well, that might not be saying much." Alex smiled.

"No, you were really smart, and your dad would come home from his visits with you full of stories about how bright you were and how proud he was of you."

Alex remembered their visits being stilted. Almost as if Crockett felt he had to be there, not that he wanted to be there. Then again, that might have had something to do with the way his mom would hover over them, never leaving Crockett alone with him. And then he'd graduated and told Crockett he didn't have time for visits anymore. He had his life to live and the time for needing a father had long passed.

A weight like a stone settled in Alex's gut. He very clearly remembered the silence on the other end of the phone after saying those words, and then Crockett had cleared his throat and wished him good luck. Alex had taken it as more abandonment, thinking the old man had given up too easily. But then he'd also been grateful that Crockett hadn't pressed.

And now he was gone forever. Had been these past five years, and Alex had barely given him a thought. That weight became a boulder.

Bill's hand landed on his shoulder. "He knew you loved him. He knew you just had your own life to live. But he'd be happy knowing you're here now. We all are."

"Not Liv so much."

"You'd be surprised what lengths Olivia will go to in order to hide her feelings when she's unsure of something."

Speaking of Liv, she knocked on the door. "Men's powwow?"

"Nope, just finishing up." Bill winked at Alex as he walked out past Liv. He stopped for a second to kiss her on the forehead. "Give him hell, Liv." And then he was gone, leaving them to stare at each other.

"Which him do you think he was talking about?" Alex asked.

"Could be you or it could be Beckham. Either works for me."

"I noticed you didn't give him the hairy eyeball or a talking to for using the swear word."

She shrugged. "It's Bill. He knows the limits and toes the line as often as possible. It keeps things lively around here." She stuck her hands into the back pockets of her jeans.

At least he didn't feel overdressed.

"You ready to head out? I'd like to get this over with."

"Did you want me to talk with Davey first and get the names?"

"I'd be lying if I said I didn't want to know who really did the damage," she said. "But then the more I thought about it I wondered if we shouldn't just leave it alone. I don't want to make waves in the community, and the cleanup is already done."

"Are you scared of retribution?"

She looked everywhere but at him.

"Come on, Liv. You wanted those names as much as I did, more even, and now you're backing down."

"It's not always rainbows and smiles around here, Alex. Sometimes people want this whole place to close because they don't want these kinds of kids hanging in their sleepy town. They don't want to face the fact that not every child has it easy, and they don't want the outside world to touch them. Having a bunch of kids like ours here makes them uncomfortable. As you've seen, there are plenty of people who help out and love these kids, but there are still many in the surrounding towns who would be happier if we didn't exist."

"Has it always been like that?"

She sent him a look of disbelief. "Yes, all the way back to when your family first started this place."

And his dad had been trying to keep the family tradition alive, knowing that these kids needed a refuge, but his mom had made that hard for him every possible time she could. Alex hadn't always heard exactly what the arguments were about, but knew his mom wanted his father to shut down the program and start up a spa or a vacation spot where executives could relax.

They'd stop talking when they saw him, so he never got any farther than that, but his mother had sung show tunes all the way to Maryland. As if she hadn't just left the life he'd known for so many years. Or at least as if she were escaping a life she hated. And he'd gone along with her because he'd wanted to stay but Crockett hadn't fought for him.

Fortunately Davey ran into his room, allowing Alex to put that whole thing on a mental shelf for a time later when he was alone. Right now they had some alpacas to buy and some names to hand over.

****

"Thank you, Mr. Beckham." Liv held her sweating glass of sweet tea in her hand, trying hard to process the facts that Beckham was going to let Davey keep the alpacas for ten dollars and that he wasn't mad at all. She had at least expected some sharpness from the perpetually grumpy man, but nothing.

"I'm glad they're going to have a good home. You'll take care of them, right, boy?" he asked Davey.

"Absolutely, sir. They'll have all the things they need, plus some. I want to raise alpacas when I get older. This will be a good start."

Liv had heard him talk about it a few times but always thought it was like little boys wanting to be firemen or astronauts. She'd had no idea he was truly serious about it. She sneaked a peek at Alex to see how he felt about having an alpaca farm started on land that wasn't even theirs. He just smiled.

"We'll get you a business plan, Davey," he said, after a moment. "You'll be the youngest, most prosperous alpaca herder the world has ever known." Alex ruffled her boy's hair.

"Glad that's settled," Beckham said. "Just keep those buggers over on your side of the fence." He stood from his recliner and led them outside to the porch. "That was brave of you to come over and tell me, Davey, but make sure you don't ever have to tell me anything like that again. You get one free pass and that's it. Ask Alex about that."

He waved them off and returned to the house.

"We didn't tell him the names of the kids who actually did the damage," Liv said as they stepped off the porch and headed down the road with Davey between them. Davey had told them he only knew one kid for certain and the others he only guessed since they all hung out together. Of course the one kid he knew belonged to the local attorney.

"There's a couple of ways we might want to handle that," Alex answered. "I think we might be able to wait just a little bit so we can celebrate Davey's new business venture first, don't you?"

She looked over at him smiling at her kid as Davey went on and on about all the things he'd do with and for his new animals. He wanted to get another one and maybe start breeding, though he wasn't sure exactly what was involved in that. When he asked her, she told him they'd discuss it later. He rambled again, mostly talking to Alex. And it was good. So good, she almost lost herself in a little daydream of having this family to call her own.

When she'd been in school, Crockett had always teased her not to get too serious about any one boy because some day Alex would come home and they'd be perfect for each other. As soon as he graduated high school, Crockett would say. And then he graduated and Crockett never left the farm again except to pick up boys from the train station.

It was a sad memory and not one fit for this afternoon when Davey was so happy and Alex looked content to be here. So she'd join in the fun and just be thankful for what she'd been given, for however long she'd been given it.

****

When they got to the house, Alex laid a hand on Liv's arm and asked her to wait, in a low voice. She gave him a weird look but did as he asked. They let Davey open the door, and the noise inside about knocked Alex back on his feet.

Everyone shouted "Congratulations!" led by Bill, who had somehow made Alex's request come to life. It was a cake with two alpacas on it and the words "Proud Dad Davey."

Liv hung back for a moment with her hand over her mouth. Alex gave her roughly one second, then grabbed her arm and tugged her along. "I know you probably weren't ready to be a grandma just yet, but at least you'll have practice for when real grandkids come along."

Her chuckle was watery, and he let it go. He didn't need to know why she was emotional, he only needed her to get into the fun of the party and then she'd be happy again. He had come to realize how much he really didn't like to see her upset and would do nearly anything to keep that smile on her face.

After the celebration, it was time to get the barn outfitted for the new arrivals. All the kids pitched in, and so did Alex and Liv. Bill begged off, saying he had to make dinner, and they let him.

Time flew by and it was soon time for dinner. Alex led them in the thankful portion of the evening. It was something Crockett had instituted years ago, and he was happy Liv had kept it. They went around the table with each one giving one good thing that had happened to them today. When they got to Davey, Alex was sure he was going to talk about how he loved his new alpacas.

"I'm thankful for the trouble we had so that Alex could come out here," the kid said instead. And for the third time that day Alex was nearly knocked off his feet.

Especially when everyone started cheering and Bill came out with Shoofly Pie. Alex hadn't had one of those in years and years.

Each boy smiled at him as Alex looked around the dining hall. They were all genuine, open, and welcoming. And almost more than he could take. He said thank you, then shoved pie into his mouth so he didn't have to say any more. He escaped as soon as he could, saying he had to shower before the boys hogged all the hot water. Then he sat in his room for a few moments. What was he still doing here? He needed to leave before he got in too deep.

Liv knocked on the door not long after he sat down. He thought about ignoring her, but it wasn't to be, when she knocked again. "Davey's looking for his business manager and wants you to help bang a bottle of sparkling apple cider against their stall door," she said through the door.

He could shower later. He had a budding businessman to celebrate with.

Chapter Eleven

Archery lessons, metal work, and whittling were the three things that made Liv cringe when it was time to do them. It wasn't that she didn't trust the boys or the instructors, but she always had stress dreams about everything that could go wrong while they were loosing arrows on hay bales or using sharp knives to make a block of wood into a kitschy ornament.

But she trusted the people who volunteered their time to come and teach the boys skills that would expand their worlds. She couldn't deny them the opportunity to learn what a knife could be used for that didn't involve stabbing. She also couldn't deny them the chance to see what they could make with their hands if given the right tools. But tonight, after they'd all worked together setting up Davey's new animals and had dinner, they headed to bed.

With the new day, it was time for new things.

As she walked from her cottage to the barn, she wondered if she should maybe make the side of the barn a mural. They'd never done anything like that before, but some of the incredible artwork from the boys at the Beckhams had really taken her breath away.

Art had been something she had toyed with bringing to the camp for a while. They had rudimentary art, like drawing trees and farm animals, but these kids had some serious skill and probably limited patience for learning things they already knew instinctively. She'd have to ask around to see if there was anyone local who would be willing to take on another volunteer position. She'd tapped nearly everyone in town, but surely there was one more person with something to give and a little time each summer to give it.

Taking her notebook out of her pocket, she wrote herself a note. She was in the process of putting the slim pad back into her pocket when Alex came strolling out of the barn with a smile on his face and his hands cupped in front of him like he had a secret.

"Do you know how long it's been since I've seen baby barn kittens?"

"Isn't that an oxymoron? Aren't all kittens babies?" she asked.

"Don't ruin this moment for me, Jameson, or I'll bring up the dreaded incident from yesterday morning that you would probably rather not talk about."

"So, a baby kitten, that's great."

He brought his cupped hands near, and she couldn't help but smell the early morning shower on him and a scent that was all his own.

But then he opened his hands, and nestled in the love and life lines on his big palm was an orange tabby that hadn't even opened its eyes yet.

A soft gasp escaped her as she used just her index finger to stroke the soft fur of the kitten's head. She hadn't felt a kitten in forever. She hadn't even realized they had a new litter. How long had it been since she'd checked? She was so wrapped up in running Breathe that sometimes she forgot the little things. Like this kitten.

"It's beautiful." The kitten twitched under her

finger and gave a soft little mewl. Something choked inside Liv, and she felt like an idiot. It was a kitten. But it was such a cute kitten, and it embodied things that she would have to pay more attention to.

"Do you want to hold him?" Alex asked, holding the feline out to her. She finished slipping the notepad into her pocket, then held out her hands in a cup. He deposited the cat into her waiting hands, brushing the backs of his fingers against the sensitive skin of her palms.

Another mewl and the kitty was safely in her hands. She couldn't resist bringing him closer to her body and feeling the heat of him against her cheek, the softness of all that newborn fur. It was like having a caterpillar crawling on her finger or a soft feather flitting across her face.

"He's adorable."

"You should see the other five." Alex stood back with his hands in his pockets. His fitted black T-shirt pulled tight against his chest, and the jeans he wore lovingly followed every line of his muscular thighs. And she definitely should not be looking.

Instead, she buried her face against the cat's fur and waited for the heated and hated blush to leave her face. Fortunately, one of the smaller boys, Raphael, ran up at that moment, saving her from awkward conversation laced with her own awareness.

"Miss Liv! Miss Liv! Whatcha got there?"

She bent down to the ten-year-old's level and showed him the kitten, feeling Alex's presence behind her the whole time. There were facets within this man that she hadn't realized before, and it was saying something that she was seeing them now.

"Do you like kitties, Raph?"

"No, they're mean and bite you fierce, and then you get the rabies and have to go to the clinic and get shots."

Her heart sank. But this was just one more way in which this world was so very different from the one where he was growing up. She might not be Crockett, maybe not even come close to how much bigger than life he had been, but she could share this small joy with a small boy and hope it made a difference.

"This kitty doesn't have rabies, and he's so very tiny that he doesn't have enough teeth to bite fiercely. Would you like to pet him?" She waited, with the kitten cradled against her chest, to see if Raphael would be enticed.

But he backed away almost immediately. "Nope."

"Come on, Raph." Alex took a step forward and stroked the kitten's head inches away from Liv's breast.

She could feel heat on her skin and didn't know whether it was from the cat or from Alex. It would be better if she didn't feel it at all.

"See, he's not going to hurt me. He's just a little thing. His eyes are even closed." Alex petted the cat for a few more seconds, then looked at the child again. "Give me your hand. I'll show you how it's done."

Raph seemed to be considering taking flight. Alex put his hand out and waited him out. And that waiting paid off when the child finally put his hand in the man's and had his first touch of a kitten's new fur.

He squeaked and then couldn't get enough. Other boys came over to see what the commotion was about and ended up crowding around to touch the tabby. Alex walked off at some point, and Liv wondered what had made him go away, trying not to be disappointed that once the boys showed real interest he had lost his.

But before the thought could firmly take hold, he was back with another two kittens cradled in his arms, accompanied by Barry, the stable guy, with two others cradled in his big muscular arms. By this time they were swarmed with kids from eight to seventeen who wanted to see these little creatures.

She'd always showed them the horses and the cows, but hadn't thought to have them be a part of the smaller animals. Something new was always good, and the fact that it came through Alex would have made Crockett proud.

****

Alex stood with one black-and-brown cat in the palm of each hand and didn't know when he had last felt so fulfilled. These kids were starved for something he was providing. Even if it was this small, they were still loving it.

When he chanced a look over at Liv, she was smiling at him like it was his first recital and he'd managed to hit all the right keys on the piano. Was this the feeling she got to experience every day? He had to say it put a pall on boardroom meetings and soulless talks over drinks in swanky bars.

One of the older guys, probably about sixteen or so, hung back but kept inching forward every few seconds. Alex decided to be bold and call him out.

"Hey, Ronnie!" he said, making his voice a little bigger and his smile too. Just as he hoped, the kid turned to him. "Do you mind taking over here for a second? My cell is ringing in my pocket. I need to make sure it's not important." He didn't give the kid much chance to say no when he handed over a ball of fur and with it about seven other kids.

That was pretty damned smart of him, he congratulated himself, until he got the hairy eyeball from Liv. Well, let her think what she wanted to. He knew there was no phone call and he knew what he was doing. He wasn't Crockett's kid for nothing, after all.

****

"Of all the stupid things," Liv grumbled under her breath low enough that none of the excited younger children around her could hear her. Alex had the perfect opportunity to get into the midst of things and had thrown it away for a phone call he didn't even appear to be taking. She wanted to throttle him.

"Hey, Miss Liv, Ronnie got to hold the kitten. Can I?" a second-year boy asked, pointing at the older kid to whom Alex had handed over one of his kittens.

She couldn't say no, but saying yes would mean that everyone in her group would be jostling for a turn. Too bad they didn't have any more kittens. "I'll agree to it if you all agree to take a turn nicely and pass the baby on without fighting when your turn is over."

Everyone's eyes gleamed at her and shone with innocence. Of course they all meant to honor their word. At least until someone had the kitten and didn't want to let it go, thinking the rule didn't apply to him.

Then the fights would start and the tears would flow—or the punches would, depending on who didn't get their way. She'd stand back and watch and only step in if it got out of hand. She handed her furry kitten over to Kevin, explained how to hold it, and made sure he was doing okay, then stepped out of the way. She didn't want them to think she didn't trust them, but she also didn't want a hurt kitten on her conscience.

Without truly thinking about it, she positioned herself next to Alex, sidling up to his left and tapping him on the arm. "Your phone call was so important you didn't even have to take it?"

He jumped a little, which was gratifying to her. But he also recovered pretty quickly. "How do you know it wasn't a text message or an email? I could have already taken care of it, all with the touch of my fingers on the screen."

Considering her cell phone was used only to make and take phone calls, she wasn't sure what all a fancy phone could do. Quite frankly, she didn't care. He had said that he was taking a phone call and had just lied to her boys. They weren't stupid, either. One of them would notice, and any trust or points Alex had gained would immediately be forfeited. That would be a shame, even if he was only planning on being here for a couple more days. These boys deserved to be able to trust anyone they came in contact with here at Breathe.

"I don't care what you were doing," she said in a low angry voice. "We do not ever lie to the boys, or try to skip out on something we're doing with them, unless it is life or death. Was your email or text life or death?"

He shrugged his broad shoulders and at least had the grace to look a little sheepish. "It wasn't a phone call, or an email, or a text. I just thought it would be good to include one of the boys who seemed to be standing back. He wanted to join in, I could tell, but he didn't know how. I gave him an in, and instant popularity, without embarrassing him or making him feel like I had singled him out. I remember Crockett doing that. It worked wonders every time."

She couldn't argue with that, but, oh, how she wanted to. "Why don't you leave this kind of stuff to me?" She had thought she could trust him to do right by the kids even if he couldn't commit full time.

"Now, wait just a minute there."

Some of the kids were turning their way and losing interest in the cats when there was obviously some kind of drama going on right near them. A lot of these kids had drama radars that she just couldn't fathom.

"Please, can we not do this here?" She said it in a near whisper, hoping to get his attention and keep him from blurting anything out. "I would rather not ruin this experience for any of the smaller ones if we can help it."

He backed off. "Lead the way. I'll follow you wherever you go."

"This way, then." She stopped for a second to let Barry know where they were going and to walkie-talkie Marcy and ask her if she could come out and help with the kittens for just a little bit. Lunch was far enough away that the other woman jumped at the chance to escape the hot kitchen for a little bit and get outside.

Once she showed up, Liv took her leave after explaining to everyone that she and Alex were going to take care of some company stuff and would be back soon. She also reminded them that archery started in twenty minutes and she didn't want to hear they had missed it.

And then they were away from the crowd.

"Why do I have the feeling you're about to take me to task for something?"

He took the wind right out of her sails. She didn't want to be the heavy, but if he was going to be here for the next little while, then he had to know how they worked and that certain things were unacceptable no matter how good his intentions were.

She led him down a path to the right of the house, out to the garden where they grew vegetables for salads and for the boys to learn about taking care of living things that depended on them.

"I'm not going to mince words, since it's obvious you know I'm not happy."

"Yeah, the cute crease in your forehead would have been my first clue if it weren't for your tone of voice and the doom-and-gloom look in your eyes. So just spit it out. What did I do that was terrible enough for you to have to reprimand me away from everyone else and make it look like it's some kind of meeting?"

Now she felt bad, because if she was going to call him out for doing the exact thing she was doing, then that made her no better.

"I'm not calling you on the carpet. I just want to remind you of a few rules we have around here."

He stood with his arms folded over his chest and a shuttered look on his face. She much preferred the awed look he'd had when he brought out that kitten. She didn't want to make him regret that he had finally made an effort to get involved, but she also couldn't allow him to undo a lot of what she had tried to do in the last three days.

"As I've said before, we absolutely do not lie to the boys, ever, no matter what it is. If you lose their trust, then you lose them altogether. I'm not willing to do that. Especially for something as small as a fake phone call. They have had a lot of lies and broken promises in their lives up to this point. For some, this is the one safe place left for them. I won't take that away, no matter if you were doing it for a good reason or not."

"Okay."

"That's it? Okay?" She was the one now standing with her arms folded over her chest. Didn't he get the importance of what she was saying?

"Yep, just okay. I'm a fast learner. If you don't want lies, even if they help the situation, then I won't tell any more. How would you have handled that, though? If you didn't know the boys and wanted to start a bond with them, how would you have gotten him over to hold the kitten?"

He seemed truly interested, which was another first. He had never been interested in anything having to do with Breathe, not since he was thirteen, as far as she knew. And now all of a sudden he seemed to want to pull it into his system and make it part of him. Which was the true Alex, and which could she trust?

She was going to go out on a limb here and see if she could trust the one she had wanted to appear for Crockett back before he passed away. She only hoped her trust wasn't going to bite her in the butt.

"Our first and foremost rule is not to lie to them. Even if it seems like a little white lie, it could mean the difference between them trusting you and them never trusting you again, even if you say the sky is blue. A lot of them come from homes that have no trust and no one who cares about them. Crockett always wanted Breathe to be the one place they could come and be kids no matter how old they are."

Alex looked back at her as if he was really listening. Still, she felt like she was lecturing him.

Who did she think she was? Yes, she ran this place,

but she ran it for him. And he had grown up here, even if it was only until he was thirteen. He had to know how some of this worked.

"Am I going over familiar ground?" she asked, hesitating to sound like she knew it all and he needed to be taught even if he knew it too.

"Actually, you're not. I wasn't very involved with anything here for a while before we actually left. My mother was against it for quite some time before our last day here. She didn't encourage me to take part at all. Being a teenager, I looked at it as the perfect excuse not to have to do any work. So I haven't heard this before. It's interesting to see your passion for this place, though. It comes through in your voice and your gestures."

Was he critiquing her? Seriously? But she put aside her instinctual reaction of letting her hackles rise. "The second rule is to be honest with them."

"Isn't that just restating the first rule? Not that I mind, since that makes the rules much easier to follow if they're really the same, but I'm just asking." His cheeky smile popped out on his face, but she didn't join him this time.

"No, actually, it is a totally different rule from the first one. The first one is not to lie, not to deliberately tell them something that isn't true. The second is distinctly separate because it involves any questions or information that we might not want them to have. But if they ask for it, you have to be honest to the best of your ability. Some things aren't their business, and even in that you can tell them it isn't their business, and that's the honest truth."

"So that's how you deal with the boys. Now, how

do you deal with the adults? If I ask you to dinner, will you say yes without lying and tell me honestly if you'd rather I take a hike?"

Chapter Twelve

Alex was surprised by how much he wanted Liv's answer to his invitation to be yes and to know she meant it. It was a novelty to be somewhere even the littlest lie was not tolerated. He didn't know if he'd be able to survive this kind of place on a full-time basis as she obviously did, but it was an interesting concept.

"I'll have to think about it."

He had to smile at her evasion. But he wasn't going to give up on pinning her down if he had to. "And why do you have to think about it? This could just be a dinner between a boss and the director of the boss's camp property to make sure we aren't interrupted while we talk about very important things having to do with said camp."

"And I don't like the way you phrased that, since it's even vaguer than I was being." Her mulish expression was not boding well for him. He was so used to playing the game in DC that he didn't know if he could turn it off without some serious readjusting. But surprisingly, he found he might be willing to give it a go. For her. Whatever that meant regarding the larger scheme of things.

"All right, look. I'd like to go out to dinner with you. I'm sure we'll talk about the camp, and yes, I would like to discuss the logistics of how everything is working and see if there are ways for us to streamline.

We might even talk about what you've been doing out here in the back of nowhere for all these years when you could have been making it big somewhere. I'd also like to know what your favorite color is, and what kind of flowers you prefer to get on your birthday, but I figure I could ask those questions at another dinner."

Her eyes got wider with every other word. He couldn't say that didn't thrill him just a little. She had never been in the game, which would be refreshing. There would be no posturing, no trying to see and be seen by the best people of the moment, no trying to pull in favors.

"Your honesty leaves a little to be desired." She huffed.

"Which parts?"

"If you don't know, I'm not going to tell you. But I will tell you this. I will go out with you for dinner, and we can talk about everything and anything you think you want to know, but in return you have to agree to teach the boys about cartooning before you go."

Shock ran through his brain and at the last second he caught the swear word that wanted to fly out of his mouth. "Wow, talk about hitting in the solar plexus. What made you bring that up?" He should have merely thought the question in his head so he wouldn't have her special brand of truth-telling thrown in his face, but he'd been taken off guard.

"Crockett framed quite a few of your drawings and the comic book you put together. They're in the study. He always hoped maybe you would make that a priority in your life."

He had to be the only person in the whole world whose father would have been happier if he was a poor starving graphic novel illustrator than a high-powered broker in Washington, DC. No wonder his mother had pulled him out before things got out of hand even more.

But the challenge of it called to his blood just a bit. He hadn't picked up the tools of framing a graphic in a very long time. It would be nothing to do it again.

"And…"

"There's an 'and' here?" he said.

"Oh, yeah, there's an 'and.' You think I'm just going to traipse off into a restaurant with you without some guarantees?"

"That's kind of how going out for dinner runs. Not a whole lot of contingencies and rules and whatever."

"Well, when it's dinner with me, expect the whatever."

"Fine, tell me the guarantee you want. But you only get one."

"Guarantee me you won't turn into a pumpkin at midnight."

He burst out laughing before he could stop himself. "You got me. I promise not to turn into a pumpkin at midnight."

"Fair enough. When?"

"How about the day after tomorrow? We have the barn to finish tomorrow, and then the annual cook-off the next afternoon. It'll be the last thing before I leave. A little saying goodbye."

She walked backward as she walked away from him. "You realize this dinner is going to be very expensive for you?"

"I can take it. No worries."

"You say that now, but just you wait."

He couldn't wait.

****

The next day dawned bright and early. The supplies came in on a seven a.m. truck, and Alex was outside already when Liv stepped out from her cottage.

"Ugh, eager much?" she asked when she saw him without even a coffee cup in his hands.

"I'm ready to get this project done for Beckham. I'm not sure what I want to do about the name Davey gave us, but I still have a few days to think about it. Getting the rest of the barn fixed will be the thing that closes it out, and I appreciate all our boys for agreeing to this. Heck, they've already eaten and are talking about those drawing classes you apparently told them about last night."

She grinned, not ashamed at all that she'd made sure there was no way he'd be able to back out of it. There was so much talent here just waiting to be tapped, and as far as she knew he could help. At least while he was here.

The boys came out on the porch behind her with Uncle Bill trailing behind them. "Everyone's ready except you. Here's your breakfast so you can get on your way."

He actually handed her a paper bag and expected her to get in the car. Okay, then, apparently she was the one falling behind today.

They took the van and the car and another car to the farm so they could haul all the supplies. Most of the same crowd was there from the first time they'd fixed the barn. Yet there were new faces, and one in particular was the lawyer's kid.

She kept Davey behind her, not sure why the boy and his father were here.

Beckham met them at the stairs. "We have some new recruits this morning. Thanks for coming, everyone. Let's get the supplies and get to work. Mrs. Beckham's been working since last night on a chicken pot pie that's going to make your mouth sing."

Beckham smiled and winked at Liv. She hung back when everyone else scattered. "How? Should I worry about Davey when he goes back to school?"

"Course not, sweetie. The boys and their fathers showed up about fifteen minutes ago, said they were doing some community service and they'd like to help get the place together. I didn't want to turn them away." He winked again and then walked away from her.

But then he turned back. "And don't forget I want some of those older boys to come back once they graduate. I've got a lot more jobs than just working hands around here, and I don't have anyone who's going to want my farm when I go. Who knows what will happen to this old homestead. Should be in some good hands, as far as I'm concerned." Then he did walk away, whistling to himself.

Liv stood like a statue, rooted to the spot. Had he called the boys' fathers and told them to get them down here? Or had he been more subtle? She'd bet on the subtle, the wily old man. And so he got the sweat from the ones who'd done the damage without confronting a single person.

She laughed and was still chuckling when Alex joined her.

"You planning on working today, or are you just here in a supervisory capacity?"

She leaned into him for a moment, shoulder to shoulder. "Just enjoying the community coming

152

together like this. That's all."

"Well, I'm sure they'd love for you to jump in."

So she did.

****

The glow on Liv's face would last him for days. He had talked with Beckham and asked him to approach the fathers to get the kids here. No one had said a word about the damage other than to talk about what needed to be fixed next. They played it off as community service for their college applications, but those kids were fully aware they'd been caught and this was their punishment.

He watched Liv interact with everyone. From their boys to the town kids, she treated them all with respect, smiles, and gratitude. No one got the cold shoulder or a harsh word. How was it that even with her losses and the huge responsibility of the farm she was so happy all the time?

"Entranced" wasn't a strong enough word for how he felt. She enthralled him, and he couldn't allow that. The kiss they'd shared, the way she fit against him when he hugged her, the way she made him think of a future in the country—it all had to be shut out of his brain.

He didn't belong here, had never belonged here. But if anything, he could thank her for giving him memories of Breathe that were no longer as sad or filled with anger.

Calling his mother sat on his mind, but he wasn't ready to deal with her yet. Betty had shared that his mother was dissatisfied long before they'd left. The older woman was apologetic about the information, as if it were her fault. He knew it wasn't, but right now he just wanted to enjoy his last few days here. Dealing with his mother could wait until he was back home.

Liv approached him with that smile, her hands in her pockets. "Now who's in the supervisory position?"

"Nah, just taking a break and watching how everything here works like a well-oiled machine. Our boys are doing an amazing job with the painting and repairing. Crockett could not have picked a better director for Breathe."

She blushed, and he found it endearing.

"I picked this for myself and followed him around whenever I could. I wanted to be the manager to his director and worked hard to make sure he thought of me when he realized he needed some help."

"He still picked well. You're a natural."

"Hey, you're pretty good at this yourself." She shrugged her shoulder into his again. If the whole town wasn't within fifty feet of them, he might just have given in to the urge to make sure her lips really were as sweet as he remembered.

The things she did to him.

He had to stop thinking like that, though, or he really might try to find some deserted hayloft and see how far he could go without losing his heart altogether.

Clearing his throat, he looked out across at all the people working. "It's a good community, and Beckham got what he wanted. I think we're all winning on this one."

"I agree. And Beckham came to me again and asked that I definitely have some of the older boys come back to help him run the farm. Do you think it might be possible to house them while they're working, if Beckham doesn't have room? The house goes empty for most of the year except for Bill, Davey, and me rambling around. Maybe we could charge them a small amount of rent so we're not losing money, but they wouldn't have to rent apartments."

"I like it. Write me up a proposal, and we'll talk about it at dinner."

"Sounds good. Now we'd better get back to work so we can earn that chicken pot pie." She brushed his hand with her fingertips and smiled up at him. His heart beat in a weird staccato from that small touch.

Hell, he might never survive a roll in the hay with her. It was a good thing he was leaving in a few days, or he might never want to leave at all.

****

The rest of the afternoon flew by for Liv. Driving one of the cars full of boys, she listened to the excited chatter about the offer from Mr. Beckham, and the pride in their voices over a job well done made her heart soar.

At least Alex seemed more open to seeing the boys in a positive light. He even seemed to have relaxed his aversion to Breathe itself. Somehow she just knew Crockett was grinning like a fool in the afterlife, smoking his cigar and crowing that he'd been right.

Well, he'd been mostly right. Alex had grown to like the camp, even calling the boys *our* boys instead of *the* boys or *the* campers or not addressing them at all. And that meant something to her. Perhaps he'd come around more now. She wasn't sure if that would be good for her heart, but Bill would be happy. And Davey, who had grown quite attached to Alex since he'd helped with his business plan and setting up the stalls for the alpacas.

When he was charming, Alex was almost too much to resist. But she had to. He was leaving, and she couldn't hope that he'd stay. It would hurt too much.

Ultimately, Crockett's dream had been for Alex and Liv to run the place together as a couple and pass it down to their children. The older man wouldn't get his whole dream, but she was pretty sure he would have been happy with what he did get.

And that was Alex, joshing around with the boys and teaching a drawing class around the campfire after they'd had s'mores. He'd upended the four boxes of art supplies Crockett had kept in his closet, hoping one day Alex would return. And he'd doled out charcoals and crayons and watercolor pencils to all the boys.

She'd looked up some of the brands online, and they were not cheap. In fact, they were top of the line. One pencil came in at almost thirty dollars, and the charcoal was costly. But he hadn't blinked as Manny asked for it and then happily sat by the fire with his tongue sticking out of the side of his mouth, drawing what he said was a kitten but looked more like a traffic cone with ears.

Everyone had headed in an hour ago, after the fire was doused. The alpacas were down for the night, the horses in their stalls, and the cows in the barn. Being this far out, they had little to no road noise, so she stood and listened to the crickets chirp and knew all was right in her world.

Tomorrow was the annual cookout, and then she'd have a goodbye dinner with Alex to discuss housing some of the boys—no, they would be men when they came back—during the rest of the year. She would enjoy the company and the time with them. It was a program she'd thought of implementing before but hadn't known how to approach it or if it would even work.

Now she had a budget and a projected output on her computer in the cottage and was ready to discuss it with Alex. He wasn't exactly a partner, but she at least felt like she had him in her corner now, whereas before she'd felt like they were just a burden that he'd taken on because he had to.

His visit had changed some things for the good. Even Bill was pleased and had thanked her for not letting her attitude out. Silly man, she *had* let her attitude out, but Alex was man enough to take it, and she appreciated that.

And him.

Too much, to be honest.

With that thought in her mind, she went to bed and dreamed of things she shouldn't dream about. Partnerships that were more than partnerships and having someone to not only stand with her but to love her and cherish her and work with her, side by side, as they made this place all it could be.

And if the L word came up in those dreams, falling from his lips as he asked her to be more than his director, then she forced it out of her mind when she rolled out of bed the next morning.

They had a cook-off to make happen and vendors who'd be by to set up in three hours.

When she stepped out of her cottage, she found Alex already up and chipper, helping people set up tents and tables.

Bill had breakfast on a set of picnic tables while he wore a ridiculous chef's hat and flipped pancakes on a griddle set up over the grill at the back of the house.

"Is this an all-day event now?" she asked her uncle.

"Sure is. Alex told people to come by for breakfast and help out with set-up so we could get into the fun sooner. He has some really good ideas about making us more money for the year by expanding the cost and the availability." Bill flipped a row of pancakes and then raised squinted eyes to her. "I hope you'll at least listen before you go off telling him you know how to do your job around here and don't need him to tell you what to do."

"I'll behave."

"Why would you start now?" Alex asked from her left.

She couldn't help the warm blush that started at her neckline. How long had he been standing there?

"I like you just the way you are, sass and all." Alex flipped the end of her ponytail as he strode by her, directing Walter and Joe with yet another table.

"You know he'd be good for you, girl. Good *to* you, too," Bill said quietly.

"I do know, Uncle Bill, but I can't have another man who's always gone or who always wants to be gone. The camp's newness and fun will wear off when it comes time to close for the winter and do all the accounting and going through applications. Plus, he has a life of his own in the city, and we can't compare to that out here."

"So you're not going to try?"

"No, he hasn't said anything to make me think he'd be open to it. And I don't want to beg again. Last time I got Davey out of the deal, but I don't think I could survive being left again."

"Not all men go." He stroked her arm.

She hugged him to her. "I know that. You've never left me, and I can't tell you how much I appreciate it. If nothing else, this has shown me I'm willing to think about dating again."

Bill's eyes gleamed.

"Do not even start setting me up on blind dates or whatever that twinkle means. I said I'd think about it. In my own time. But some day Davey will be grown, and I'd like someone to share my life with, I think. Maybe." She smiled. "Another day. Right now, I smell barbecue, and it looks like Candace brought out her handmade necklaces. I love those things."

She waved to Bill and walked away. What would it be like to have Alex here all the time? She could see him going into the city as necessary. She'd have plenty to do here, and even if he was gone a few days a week, it wouldn't be a problem. At the thought of being able to spend time with him and possibly make a life with him, she found she was willing to compromise on a lot. But there was no way to compromise if the other person wouldn't meet you halfway. Heck, especially if they weren't even on the same road as you.

Alex had just gone from hating this place to tolerating it. She couldn't expect him to love it like she did. She couldn't expect him to love her like she knew she loved him, not when he had so much to work through after years of resentment.

She understood that and could wait. Maybe it would happen some day. In the meantime, though, she was going to start living for more than just the camp. But first she was going to have dinner with Alex and see what happened from there.

Chapter Thirteen

For the last fifteen minutes Liv had been staring at her closet wondering when was the last time she had gone anywhere that she had to wear something besides jeans, shorts, or sweats. She had the one black dress she wore if there was a funeral in the community, but other than that, she had nothing. Or at least nothing that fit. A few things hung in the back of the closet that she'd worn when she'd first gotten married, but she was no longer that skinny little nineteen-year-old, and they were all hopelessly out of fashion, anyway.

How could yesterday's cook-off have been such a success, and she was thanked and thanked again by everyone, and yet today she felt like a terrible failure? They'd raised over ten thousand dollars for the boys, with games and vendor tables and food. She was an astute business woman and a success at her job.

In the department of being just a woman, though, she was coming up lacking.

Slumping back on the bed, she stared at the ceiling. There was no way she could pretend this was just going to be a business dinner. No way to liken it to their business ice cream. This was actual dinner, and she was going to have to go shopping if she had any hope of not looking like a country bumpkin. It was time to call in the troops.

After letting Bill know she'd be back in an hour or

so, she met Maddie at the local thrift store and hoped against hope they'd have something that would fit her. She could have driven another twenty minutes to a department store, but she didn't always like the things they had on the rack, and the prices were hard to stomach when she knew she'd probably never wear the thing again. It would just hang in the back of her closet for the next ten years until maybe someone else asked her out after her son was an adult.

That was a depressing thought, so she shut it down as she waved to Maddie and parked her car.

"Shopping!" the very pregnant Maddie squealed. "You never ask to go shopping. I don't even get to go with you for jeans anymore since you know exactly what you want, what size you want, and then you order them off the internet. So boring."

"And this is not going to be very exciting. I just need a nice pants suit, and then we'll get going."

"A pants suit? Huh?" Maddie said incredulously. "Absolutely not. I don't care what you're doing, you're not wearing a pant suit."

Skirting around the edges of her own rule about lying, Liv had not told Maddie exactly where she was going or who she was going with. She'd said business dinner and left it at that. It might come back to bite her in the butt at some point, but she was willing to risk it to just get this over and done with.

"There is nothing wrong with a good pants suit. Not everyone can wear the frilly sundresses you like."

And today's was stunning. It had beautiful big orchids on it and the hem hit her right at the knee. With her big pregnant belly, Maddie looked like she could have graced the cover of a magazine. Liv often thought that her only hope for a magazine cover photo was if she got picked to stand with a cow on the back of the *Farmers' Almanac*.

"Well, you are not wearing a pants suit, and I refuse to help you buy one. Anything you pick out like that I will make a mockery of in the middle of the store. Loudly. And you know how everyone listens to pregnant women."

Liv thought hard about just walking back to her car and finding a nicer shirt to pair with her jeans. Maddie grabbed her arm and dragged her into the store instead. Not only did you have to listen to a pregnant woman, you apparently also had to follow her wherever she was taking you.

Liv waved to several of the women in the store. She shopped here for the boys sometimes if they hadn't come with enough clothes. There was a closet on the second floor of the house at Breathe stocked for every size of boy she'd ever run across. And all in solid colors. She had had several boys come one year with vulgar T-shirts and had to put her foot down and change them out. And by the time they'd left, they didn't want to take the shirts back with them.

She did good work there, and at least it seemed Alex was getting the gist of that. It was the one positive about him sticking around until the rest of the supplies arrived. There were other positives, but she wasn't going to think about them right now or she'd end up blurting something out to Maddie and starting a train of conversation she was not willing to ride.

"Dresses, Annmarie! We need dresses!" Maddie sang to the owner of the store for any person in the whole store to hear.

"We do not need dresses, Maddie, and you don't need to announce it to the whole store," Liv whispered furiously.

And that was the wrong thing to say.

Maddie peered at her and dragged her over to one of the chairs outside the fitting room. "I don't believe you ever told me exactly what this dinner was for or who it was with."

"It's nothing, with no one special."

"Lies! Lies, I tell you!" Maddie said dramatically. Everything was dramatic when she was pregnant. Liv should have remembered that. Instead, she was now the center of all the attention in the whole store.

"Keep it down, before anyone comes over."

"I will not keep it down until you tell me who this dinner is with and where you're going. Surely we can find something here to fit the occasion and the date." Maddie shot her a sly look, and Liv was defeated. Her best friend already knew who, or Maddie wouldn't have been so sure of herself. And just like that, everyone in the store came over—from the clerks to the other ladies shopping—and Liv was surrounded.

This was why she stayed out at the farm so much and did her clothes shopping online for herself. Fewer questions and fewer interactions. She'd happily take one for the team to get the boys clothes, but when it came to her personally, she did not like to talk about herself or ask for help.

"I'm going to dinner with Alex to discuss the camp. It's not a big deal and it's just a business dinner. But I think we're going into Harrisburg, and I didn't want to be underdressed, in case he decides to go to something besides the local pizza place on the corner of

Fifth and Forrester."

"A date with Alex?" Maddie laid her hands over her heart. "A real date?"

"No. I just told you. It's not a real date. It's dinner to discuss business." But she was talking to no one but herself in the mirror. Everyone else had scattered and was busy moving hangers over the racks. The noise was almost deafening with the *click-click-click* of the hangers moving back and forth across the metal poles. How many dresses were there in this place? She should have just made do somehow with what she had at home.

Rising from her chair, she thought to sneak back out to her car and leave them to their frenzy of shopping. But Maddie shot her a look across the store that had her rooted to the floor. She wasn't going anywhere. She might as well just sit down and let them try to dress her. She'd buy whatever they picked for her and then go home and dress in jeans and a nice shirt. If Alex wanted to go somewhere fancy, he could just change his mind and pick somewhere that jeans were welcome.

A half hour later, Liv would have sworn she'd tried on every dress in the entire store, not to mention skirts and even pants and dress shirts against Maddie's advice. Barbara Stapleton had pulled out this outfit in taffeta that had a jacket and pants in a teal color with black accents. Liv hadn't had the heart to tell her that the last time that style had been in was thirty years ago, so she tried it on and was happy to be able to get out of it when Maddie told her no.

With only a few dresses left, Liv almost felt bad that she hadn't found anything to make everyone happy. She was also tired of taking shirts and skirts and clothes in general on and off. She hadn't undressed and redressed this much in her whole life.

If she didn't find something here, at least she'd already made up her mind to wear something more casual.

"I know you're not going to want to try this on, but I just found it in the back, and it's marvelous."

Liv eyed the sundress with its narrow shoulder straps and asymmetrical hem. The colors were bold and reminded her of the sea—blues and greens, with aqua and hints of gray bled through in an almost watercolor look. It would be horrendous on her, but she'd try it on anyway, just so she could get out of here. Her hour was almost up, and if she saw another dress in the next ten years it would be too soon.

She took the thing into the dressing room and kept her eyes averted. There was no need to see the way the material expanded around her hips or fell to that weird place on her legs that made her look like her torso was a tree trunk. Pulling the fabric so that it settled around her chest more comfortably, she opened the door and prepared to hear that this one again wasn't right for her.

"Oh." Maddie clapped her hands to her mouth. "Oh," she sighed.

"Right, so this one is wrong, too, and I have at least one nice shirt at home that will look okay paired with jeans, or I can even wear my funeral dress if I have to. It's a business dinner. Alex isn't going to care what I look like."

Liv went to close the door. She hadn't even made it all the way out of the dressing room this time. Which was fine with her. She knew herself and knew her place. It was at Breathe in jeans and tennis shoes, T-shirts and jeans or shorts. Not dressed up for a night on the town.

Maddie grabbed her arm and dragged her out into the middle of the floor. A collective gasp went up to the rafters of the place.

"So it wasn't enough for you to see how bad I look in this, you had to give everyone else a gander too?" Liv grumped and tried to go back to the dressing room.

"You are stunning," Annmarie said, her fingers on her chin as she circled Liv.

"This dress is amazing." Jean Righthold said, circling behind Annmarie.

With a huge smile on her face, Maddie joined the circle along with the three other women who were helping with the dressing of Liv.

She felt like she was playing that game Caught in the Circle that she sometimes played with the younger kids. No one was holding hands in this circle, though, and she could have gotten out without breaking their hold, but she felt caught in the middle of something bigger than herself. She wasn't sure she really wanted to get out.

"You're lovely."

"You look amazing."

"Stunning, sweetheart."

"Absolutely amazing."

At this point, Liv had no idea who was saying what, but she was going to cry if they kept it up. Someone handed her shoes. She slipped them on and they were a perfect fit. She felt like Cinderella and Pretty Woman all wrapped into one.

Maddie seemed to read her mood and see how

close to the edge she was. "Okay, ladies, let's let Liv get back into her own clothes so she can get on the road to this dinner."

And then Liv finally looked at herself in the mirror and had to sit down on the folding chair in the corner of the curtained-off room. What was she doing? This was dinner with a man who was leaving tomorrow. Her boss, the guy who signed her checks. She did not have to look like this to go discuss business with him. And yet she couldn't stop looking at herself in the mirror. Even sitting down, the dress looked beautiful on her. Flattering in the right places, fitted in the right places, and the color, against her tan from working outside with the boys, made her glow.

Maybe she shouldn't buy it. But she was fully aware Maddie would not let her walk out of the shop without the dress and would stand in her bedroom to make sure she wore it, if need be.

And what was wrong with treating herself? What was wrong with not always being Liv the Camp Director, the mentor, the mother? What was wrong with just for one night being Liv, just Liv?

Nothing. There was nothing wrong with that. Alex better be ready to be wowed off his feet, and she was so ordering the most expensive thing on the menu. He could afford it, and she was going to enjoy herself. If this was going to be her only date in the last decade and possibly for the next decade, then she was going to live it up.

She hoped he was ready.

****

Alex tucked his folder into the trunk of his low-slung car. He was excited to show Liv the information he'd gotten from a national corporation who handled camps just like this one on a franchise basis. They could have help so Liv would have both the opportunity to not be tied to this place all the time and the funding to help expand the operation.

But that could wait until after he found out what kind of flowers she liked to receive on her birthday.

And then there she was, stepping onto the paved driveway from the little flagstone path he and his father had laid when he was ten. Crockett had wanted him to understand the importance of work and making something beautiful yet functional.

Alex did, and had used that lesson his whole life. Liv was the living breathing essence of that very concept. Where normally he saw her in jeans and T-shirts, seeing her in a dress was a whole new experience. The dress looked like one of his favorite watercolor paintings of the ocean. Liv in it paired with low heels made him feel like maybe he should roll his tongue back into his mouth.

"You clean up nice," he said before he thought better of it. He certainly could have been more suave than that. God.

But she laughed, that full, robust laugh that hit him low in the gut, and he was grateful. This was someone he could be himself with. He didn't have to watch every sentence to make sure he was saying things the right way, with the right tone and nuance to impress. With her he just was, and that was far more freeing than he had ever realized.

"I'm thinking maybe I should have been the one to make you promise you wouldn't turn into a pumpkin at midnight." He smiled, and she returned the favor.

"No pumpkin. I promise. Let's hope there aren't any little mice running around as men to open doors for us. And I'd really like to keep both these shoes after the evening."

Now it was his turn to laugh. He opened the door with a flourish and captured her hand to lower her into the car. Brushing a kiss along the backs of her knuckles made her blush. She was something else. He didn't know what, and part of him knew not to get too attached, but she was a breath of fresh air, and he craved that, no longer wanting the smog and congestion of the big city.

He hustled around the front of the car, discreetly waving to the twenty boys who were clustered into the four windows fronting the house as he got into the convertible and cranked over the engine.

On the way across the river, they laughed about Davey and his new alpacas. How he had moved the cats into his area of the barn so the other boys knew where to find them if they needed one to cuddle with. Not that they'd call it cuddling, but that was what it was.

The mama cat had tried to move them back to her place under the staircase to the hayloft, but Davey had very patiently explained to her that the back corner was their new home, and he'd take care of them. After that she left them where he'd put them along with a bowl of water and some cat food Alex had picked up in town when he went to ask Betty about the best place to go for dinner.

She'd eyed him up and down and kept her lips clamped together for a moment.

"Don't you hurt my girl," she'd finally said.

"I won't," he'd promised, and he meant it. If

anything, being out here had shown him there was so much more he should have been doing to make sure this great woman had more of a chance to live. And he had the folder in the back to prove he was making that effort to give her life back to her.

He told her about trying Betty's new avocado salsa surprise.

"Fire is probably an understatement," Liv said, laughing.

"Yeah, I'm glad you weren't there or I might have been treated to the Heimlich maneuver again."

"Hey, I thought I was saving your life."

"And doing a fine job of it."

She laughed again, and he loved it.

Once they pulled into the parking lot of the restaurant, Alex straightened his tie before he opened the door for her. Holding out his hand, he was never so thankful for having a car that was low to the ground. This way he had to help her emerge. Especially in that dress and with those heels.

When she stood up, he watched as she straightened her dress and wobbled on the heels a little. His hand under her elbow stopped the wobble and got him a smile that would light a city for months without the sun.

They were seated quickly and ordered once she had a chance to look at the menu. Laughing and joking, they made their way through appetizers and salads and the main course. The folder under his thigh on the chair was burning a hole in his leg, but he wanted to keep this personal conversation going for a just a little bit longer.

"Davey is a great kid. So much heart and honesty in one little boy."

She smiled, running her finger around the rim of

her water glass. "He's an old soul. He alternately frustrates me and fascinates me, but I wouldn't trade him for the world. I wish his dad had gotten to meet him. I think he would have been proud of him."

The smile drooped, not quite into a frown but something with a tinge of sadness and yet happiness rimmed her mouth.

"He doesn't ever see Davey? Does he live too far away?" he asked.

"Oh, no. Paul died before Davey was born."

He leaned back in his chair. She was a widow? He'd expected maybe divorce, or perhaps that they hadn't gotten married in the first place. He realized he didn't even know whether her last name was that man's last name or if she'd taken her own back after her husband died.

"I'm so sorry. I wasn't aware he had died."

"It was a freak accident. He had a brain tumor that no one knew about. He'd get headaches sometimes, but he was a truck driver, and that can happen from sitting for all those hours every day. We passed it off as things just taking a toll on his body. He'd talked about quitting and helping out with Breathe, but that didn't happen, and then he was gone. I found out I was pregnant a week later."

"That must have been terrible." He couldn't even try to imagine what turmoil she must have gone through.

She smiled softly. "It was at the time, but then my beautiful baby boy was born, and I had someone who needed me. Paul was a good man, but I don't think he ever really wanted to work with Breathe. I knew one day I was going to take over running it from your dad.

171

It was sooner than I expected, but I don't think Paul would have liked being a camp director. He had too much city in him to fully appreciate living where you can hear the crickets outside instead of in your walls."

He knew the feeling. "Was he on board with staying at the camp, if he hadn't passed?"

"For the most part. He had the open road calling him, but I was his base. It was fine."

It didn't sound fine, and she shouldn't have to only be a home base to anyone. She needed someone who thought of her first. Hell, if he lived here, he couldn't imagine going a day without seeing her.

He put a serious halt to those thoughts. He also had too much city in him to be thinking of her as anything more than his camp director. This dinner could be a moment out of time, but the fact was they would never be on the same track in life. He wouldn't live out here and she wouldn't live in Washington, DC. So they'd enjoy themselves and then he'd go home.

This seemed to be a good time to introduce the papers to her. To bring out something happy to move beyond that look on her face that told him she was about to fall into old memories that might not be all that happy.

"So I have a proposition for you."

"Sounds intriguing." She leaned her elbow on the table and then put her chin in her upturned hand. "Let me guess. You want to give me a huge raise and unlimited funds to do whatever I want to the farm."

"Cheeky, but not far from the truth."

She sat up straight in her chair. "Are you serious? I thought we were only just running in the black."

"We are, but that could all change if we partner

with this company." He brought out the folder and laid the contents on the table. He was so into his presentation of the way things could work that he totally missed her reactions. He explained how she'd have more time, and they'd have more money and could help more kids with few if any changes to the rules or core of Breathe. When he finally took a breath, he realized she had gone completely silent. When he looked up, he found her leaning far back in her chair with her arms not just folded at her chest, but her fingers digging so hard into her upper arms that the flesh had turned white around the edges.

"I'm sensing you're not on board with this," he said finally.

Her mouth dropped open. "Your deduction skills are a marvel. I only wonder why you wouldn't have used them beforehand to know that there is no way I'd be on board with giving up control to some corporation. Your father was approached by someone like that, and he didn't even let them take their coat off before he was sending them back on their way out the door."

"They have good ideas, though. And maybe you'd be able to travel some. I could show you Washington, DC. Davey would love it there. We could go to the zoo, and I could take you out for really good sushi."

"I don't eat raw fish. Ever. But that's beyond the fact that I am completely against this idea, and I'm not going to say anything more than that."

"I'm asking you to consider a way to help more boys, and you're being stubborn." He closed the folder and winged it to the side, where it almost slid off the table.

****

Liv needed a moment so she wouldn't say anything she couldn't take back. She inhaled, then exhaled. When she realized that wasn't helping, she just went with her gut. He'd either understand or not. Whichever way he went, it was good this was no more than a one-evening kind of meal. She wouldn't be able to stand him being around here all the time if this was his idea of a good idea.

"Stubborn?" She laid her napkin beside her plate. "You think I'm being stubborn? Do you think your great-grandfather wasn't stubborn for keeping that land in your family during the years when the Great Depression raged through the nation? Or when your grandfather started taking in kids off the street and had his neighbors breathing down his neck for bringing the riffraff into their tidy white community? How about your own father, who did this despite the way his wife left him for having an idea of making the world a better place? He expanded the place to what it is today, making sure these kids who suffer for a good part of the year have somewhere to come that is safe, someone to come to who is also safe. They have the ability to run and be free. They have the place and the space that you just don't get in the inner city."

His wide-eyed stare was enough to keep her going when she knew she should shut up.

"You grew up in some fancy neighborhood and probably had a park down the street and a mother who could devote herself to you after she decided she couldn't devote herself here with that same riffraff that your grandfather fought for in order to get them here. You didn't have to hope a fire hydrant broke so you could play in water. You didn't have to stay off the streets after a certain time, or think you'd better book it if there were shots fired in the neighborhood because they could be coming for you or someone in your family. These kids deal with all that and more, and some of them without a stable place to call home. Your mother took you away so you didn't have to be exposed to that kind of reality."

"Let's leave my mother out of this. You don't know the whole story of that, and I'm not going to discuss her with you." He clenched his linen napkin in his hand.

Good. She was riled up; he could be too. "You might not want to discuss it, but it should be out in the open. Crockett never said one bad word about your mother, even though he'd sit in that club chair in his office, with some board book on his lap, for hours after coming home from visiting you. Every time. So you might not want to discuss it, but there were plenty of people in town who were all too ready to fill in the gaps. Your mother thought she was marrying into money, according to them, that she was coming to a gentlemen's farm like in the South, with butlers and horses and rolling hills, where she could hold court over tea parties. And she got stuck on a working farm with boys that had to be taken care of and very little money to speak of that wasn't immediately plowed back into the farm. She wanted out, and then she found out she was pregnant."

"That's enough," he demanded.

Despite the warning voice in the back of her head, she persisted, just changed directions. "Fine, but you got me on a roll, and now you're going to get it all. Little Manny, who has the night terrors? He saw his brother get shot in the face as his father held the gun. The mother went into drug rehab, and now he's with us for the summer because they're trying to figure out which home to put him into when he gets back to Philly. He has every one of his possessions with him, and he came with a cardboard box and an old backpack on his back. He's nine."

"But this corporation has the same goals as what you have, and they have more money to do a better job of it."

It didn't escape her notice that he skipped right over the human factor. "That's crap, and here I thought you were a smart guy. They have other properties, and they might come in with the whole song and dance about keeping everything the same, but it won't be Crockett's Breathe anymore. It won't be the place where every kind of person here in town comes to volunteer and do their part. Everyone will have to go through a screening process and all schedules will have to be approved and signed and run by corporate. I won't be able to get a call from the Strocks to hear that a calf is being born and pile everyone into the van and go see the wonder of it all, because I'll need permission slips and timetables. We won't be able to do bonfires anymore because, oh, think of the sugar content in marshmallows and the unhealthiness of chocolate or the fact that a kid might burn himself."

He shook his head. "You've gone off the deep end. They are not going to make this some kind of soul-sucking institution after they pay for it. They have promised me that it will run just as it is now, with you at the helm. You will have autonomy, but you'll also be able to have some time off and a life of your own.

You'll have an assistant and someone who can solicit donations from around the country to serve these boys and their needs. You'll have the best of both worlds."

"I have the best of the world I love right now and don't need or want more."

With that she walked away, too frustrated by his pigheadedness and blindness to not say something more that she would regret later on.

Chapter Fourteen

After sitting alone at the table for fifteen minutes, Alex finally admitted that Liv must have had someone else take her home. He paid the check, then got into his car and called her cell. He'd had enough, and trying to talk with that girl was not doing his blood pressure any good. She wouldn't listen to reason nor would she see it.

But he had to admit that something about her fire and passion did spark a fire within himself. He admired her and her verve for what she was doing here, but he had to do what was best for himself too. He was thinking about these kids even if she wouldn't believe it.

When she didn't answer for the fourth time, he gunned the engine and cut out down the dark and desolate street. He could be stubborn too, and as much as his father had done everything for this camp, he hadn't done what was important for his family. So what she saw as heroic stubbornness he saw as being consumed by something that lost him everything that should have mattered more to him than a camp for boys.

Cranking the music, he decided to take the long way back to the camp so he had some time to think. There was no one and nothing waiting for him there, other than probably some emails, and those could be dealt with tomorrow.

He headed out toward the lake at the edge of town, wanting the silence and the darkness of the place. They had never put any lights out by the spot because no one wanted the blight on the landscape.

His headlights cut through the darkness that was relieved only by the moon above. But even that didn't filter through the tree branches laced together over the road to create a kind of living canopy.

He went around the bend in the road, remembering the time Crockett had made him take the corner over and over again because it was a good way to learn control of the car. He had been seven and sitting on his father's lap in an old Model T Ford. So illegal yet so vivid.

Did Liv let the boys drive farm equipment? The rules and expectations out here in Central Pennsylvania could be vastly different from those in the city. Out here, kids were expected to do whatever they could to help their families. They were close to the Amish, and those families had kids until the house was popping at the seams sometimes. But they all knew how to help out around the house and do things that city kids would never dream of doing. They all chipped in as the kids did here. He hadn't seen a cell phone in days. If there was an activity, they were all doing it. No one was left out, and no one was allowed to stay behind.

But if a corporation came in and rearranged everything to be utterly compliant with their infrastructure, would that be a bad thing?

He slowed to a crawl and pulled off at the lake. It probably would be a bad thing, and he was coming to see that after letting the conversation with Liv run back through his head.

Damn.

When Liv didn't answer her cell again, he called Bill to see if she had made it home,.

"Barry picked her up. She just came through the house, grabbed a cookie, and stalked barefooted to her cottage. You might want to let her go until tomorrow."

"I'll be home in just a minute. I'd like to talk to you when I get there."

"I'm in the kitchen like I always am."

"See you soon."

Alex took the fast way back to the farm. After pulling into the drive, he parked and took just a few seconds to calm himself. He found Bill right where he said he'd be, with hot chocolate and toast waiting for Alex on the counter.

"You didn't have to do that."

Bill shrugged his broad shoulders. "I figured if she left you at the restaurant, you didn't get a chance to have dessert. This should do instead."

Alex took his first bite of hot chocolate-covered toast after dunking, and it was better than he remembered.

"I don't think this can wait until tomorrow, Bill," he said after swallowing. "I don't feel right leaving her like that after our talk, if you want to call it a talk. I'm thinking it was more like a civilized swordfight with words."

"Liv's good at that when you get her riled. I'd go after her at your own peril, though. If you give her time, she'll calm down and talk more like a rational human being."

"I made her an offer I thought she'd love, and she

went after my mother. I think we need to clear the air on both of those."

"Ah, she didn't quite call it an offer when she came through here grumbling. It was taken more like an asinine demand of stupidity, in her own words."

Alex laughed, but it was more derisive than humorous. Her take on it didn't surprise him, not after he'd thought about it more. "I want to apologize for that. I thought I was helping and instead I insulted her. But I would like to also talk to her about my mother. She wasn't the spoiled rotten girl everyone seems to think. She had my best interests at heart and thought she was saving me from growing up in a rough environment."

Bill just stared at him with his lips clamped tight.

"What?" Alex asked.

"I'm not going to be the one to say anything."

"Come on, Bill. I can't go in blind. I'm tired of the innuendos and people talking around the subject. I didn't want to discuss it with Liv at dinner because I was hoping for something a little more intimate. But you and I have known each other for a long time. Did my mother really think she was coming to some farm with a butler and maids? Was she angry when she found out she was pregnant and thought she was stuck here for the rest of her life?"

Bill rubbed his forehead. "She wasn't happy when they pulled in the driveway the first time, and she made noises about leaving him—until she found out she was having you. That's all I'm going to say. If you want more, I'd say you should probably talk to her. I liked your mom. She had a good heart, but she could be manipulative when she wanted something she wasn't getting. And there was a lot she wasn't getting here at Breathe."

Alex sat at the island and put his head into his hands. At Bill's words, a flood of static pictures ran through Alex's mind. He loved the woman, he truly did, but Bill had it right in a lot of ways. She could get pouty when she didn't get her way, and if she expected one thing and got another, then she was not always the happiest of campers. But would she have uprooted everything because she wasn't getting her way? Make him grow up thinking his father wanted nothing to do with him except the bi-yearly obligatory visits, just because she was angry and hadn't gotten her way?

He didn't want to believe it.

"Tomorrow morning, you say?" Alex asked Bill as he rose from the chair.

"Tomorrow morning would be better than right now. If she's pissed, you don't want to get in her way."

"I'll take it under advisement."

"I loved your mom," Bill said, moving Alex's cup to the sink. "We all did, and I was heartbroken along with everyone else when she left. Even more heartbroken that she took you with her. You were my boy almost as much as you were Crockett's. Remember when we used to go fishing? You caught the littlest fish I think I'd ever seen, besides those goldfish you used to win at the carnival. But you were so pleased that we made a big deal out of your first catch. Your dad waited for you to go into the house and crow to your mom. Then he threw it back in."

"We had fish for dinner that night." Alex remembered that vividly, along with the celebration and all the congratulations.

"And I told you that you'd fed the whole family."

Alex chuckled at the memory. "I guess you're not as tight with the no-lies rule around here."

"Not unless it's really important. So I'm not going to say anything more about your mother. I don't want to lie to you, but I can't paint the prettiest of pictures for you, either. I'm just glad you're here and hope that maybe you won't stay away as long next time."

"I won't. Thank you for everything, Bill. Everything."

"Of course, boy. Now go get some shuteye. We'll see what tomorrow brings."

"Right, tomorrow. See you, Bill. Thanks for the hot chocolate and toast."

"Anytime, boy, anytime."

Alex walked out onto the back porch because he wasn't ready to call it a night yet. He needed to decide if he wanted to talk with his mom or just let that sleeping dog lie. What would he accomplish by asking her why they had really left?

And yet he'd heard so many things in the days he'd been here, and he just wasn't built to ignore it. He knew right where to get the truth. Or as much as she'd want to tell him. Because she could be manipulative when she didn't get her way and was perfectly capable of coming up with a way to get what she wanted without looking like the bad guy.

He pressed the speed dial with her face on it before he gave it any more thought. If he could find out, then at least one aspect of this would be cleared up.

"Where are you?" she asked instead of saying hello.

"I'm fine. How are you?"

"I'd be better if I knew what in the world you are up to. No one has seen you around town, and your secretary refused to tell me where you'd gone even when I told her I had an emergency. She just told me to use your cell phone number."

"And yet I have no missed call from you. Did you not really have an emergency?"

"Well, maybe not an emergency, but we were invited to the Lawsons' for dinner tomorrow night and I didn't want you to miss it. Their daughter Alexis is beautiful, smart, and well connected. You could do worse, and her daddy is a senator. This could be very good for you."

And there was the manipulation in all its glory, trying to guilt his secretary, by lying, into telling her what she wanted to know, and all because she wanted connections in town and was willing to marry him off to get them. She wasn't a bad woman in any sense, but she was used to getting what she wanted and doing whatever it took to get it.

"I'm out of town."

"Where?"

"Just out of town."

"Come on, now, Alex. Tell me where you are. You don't want your poor mother to worry about you, do you? You could be hurt, and I wouldn't even know where to have them start looking for you."

And yet she hadn't tried to call him on his cell phone, and she hadn't called his office until she wanted him to get her into a senator's house. "I'm not hurt, and I'm perfectly capable of taking care of myself. I should be home next week."

"But what about tomorrow?"

"Either you go by yourself or we can go another time. I have things to do."

"What is so important and secretive that you can't tell me?" she demanded.

"Hey, Alex, Bill wanted me to let you know that those baby chicks should be out tomorrow, if you want to show the Breathe boys," Barry said as he walked by the porch.

"Thanks, Barry," Alex answered.

There was a long stretch of total and complete silence. He waited for the explosion and wasn't surprised when it was bigger than he had thought it would be.

"Breathe! What the hell are you doing at that godforsaken place? You left me without an escort to the opera, and now you won't come home to take me to a senator's for dinner because of that horrid farm? What has gotten into you? You come home right now. Right this instant."

"I'd like to remind you that I am no longer fifteen years old. I do not need you to tell me what to do, or how to do it, or how long I can do it for."

"I'm sorry, sweetie." Her voice went down almost to a whisper. "It's just that memories of that place make me so sad, and knowing that your father chose it over you has always broken my heart. I don't want you to have to deal with that rejection and abandonment."

"And yet he left me the farm and everything on it."

"And look at what a pain that's been the past five years."

"I've barely done anything for it."

"But it's a money suck, sweetie," she said. "Think of what else you can do with that money. The things you could accomplish without having to think about that place."

"Why wouldn't I want to think about this place? I know I left when I was a teenager, but not everything about it was bad when we left."

"It was terrible, and those boys wanting to hit you, and that man I'd married barely said two words to you. He didn't even come after us."

And yet Alex knew why, now, and he believed Bill. "I have to go, Mother."

"Come home," she said.

"When I'm ready. Tell me one thing, though. When you told Crockett we were leaving, what did he say?"

"He was shocked when I called him from DC, of course. He wanted to know where we were staying and how long it would take him to get here."

His heart clenched. She hadn't even let his father say goodbye to him. "So you didn't actually tell him we were leaving. You've always said you went to his office and begged him to leave with you. He refused, telling you the camp was more important, so you packed up a few of our things and we left within ten minutes. Now you say that he didn't know we were gone until we were three hours away."

"I…" She trailed off, and he could almost see her brain working, through the phone line.

"No, please don't come up with a lie, another lie. I'll see you when I get home. Don't call me until I call you."

He hung up knowing Liv was probably way better at forgiving than he was. She might be ready to be civilized tomorrow, per Bill, but Alex wasn't sure he should talk to his mother again for at least a month if he didn't want to say things he couldn't take back.

And yet he wanted to see Liv now, to let her know he was sorry. That he shouldn't have tried to make things easier for her when she already did it all flawlessly.

Her light flipped on, and he saw her silhouette across the front curtains. Would she turn him away?

It didn't matter what she'd do. He was leaving tomorrow. He needed time to come to terms with what he'd learned tonight and to rearrange the pieces in his head. To deal with the grief he felt creeping in over all the years he'd missed with his dad. All the time he could have spent here. Maybe if he'd met Liv earlier, things would have been different. But that hadn't happened, and things weren't different. He still had a life in DC, and she still was tied to the camp and to her son.

He respected and understood that now, enough to not ask her to choose him over everything that meant anything to her.

Chapter Fifteen

Liv couldn't relax. She'd tried everything she could after she ate the cookie she'd snatched from the kitchen. Meditation just gave her too much head space to think too many things. Reading wasn't working, she realized when she'd read the same page eight times and still had no idea what was said. She'd tried a bath and that didn't help. So now she was pacing.

She shouldn't have said anything about Alex's mom. That was a low blow, and being hurt by his suggestion was no excuse to have pulled out that gun, aimed it, and shot him straight in the heart. She'd have to apologize to him. Tomorrow. She was too raw tonight to do it.

Right now she just wanted to close her eyes and go to sleep, but every time she did she thought about how his face had gone stony after her comment about his mom. A far cry from how it had been filled with light when he thought he was offering Liv a way to have more of a life, to travel, to be able to take a break from being the primary caretaker of this place. And she'd thrown it all back in his face without even giving him a chance.

She still didn't want anyone running this place but her, and all of her reasons were valid and true. She'd even looked into it once herself, thinking maybe they'd be able to help more boys. But after a lot of research she'd let the idea die. It would change the dynamics and the structure of the place she loved, and that wasn't worth it. She'd rather give all of her to the ones she could help than spread things too thin and have the experience that Crockett had lived for and loved be overshadowed by corporate guys.

But she should have said all of that to Alex instead of going right for his jugular. Bill was not going to be happy when he found out how she'd walked out on Alex. She'd explain it to him tomorrow too. Now she had to find a way to relax.

A knock sounded on her door. Peeking through the window, she saw Alex and didn't want to answer it. But he smiled at her, and she knew she'd have to.

Fortunately she hadn't yet changed into pajamas and had track pants and a T-shirt on. Better than that damn dress that had made her dream of possibilities that were never going to be.

"So Bill warned me that it would be better to approach you in the morning because it's best to give you time to get over your mad before trying to talk to you. But I guess I'm not very good at following advice."

And there it was, that smile that melted her heart. The honesty that she valued, and the way he just laid things on the line. He had his faults, but he also had a ton of good qualities.

"Thanks, and I promise not to bite your head off."

"I wanted to apologize."

"For which part?" she asked.

"Ah, so you aren't going to make this easy. Well, I guess I didn't expect anything less."

Holding the door open wider, she grinned at him.

"Do you want to come in so you can maybe grovel on your knees for my forgiveness without the boys having to watch your downfall?"

"Cheeky. I like that, and I'd like to come in, if it's okay. Because I have several things to apologize for, and it could take a little while."

"Now I'm intrigued. Do you want a snack? Some water?" She remembered she had left before dessert, but didn't mention that, since then she might have to apologize too. Actually she knew she was going to apologize but was trying to put it off for as long as possible. She wanted to see what he had to say before it got to her turn to ask for forgiveness.

"Water would be great."

"Right, to keep the throat working for all those flowery words of apology you're going to throw at me."

"Something like that."

She got him a glass, then took a seat on the chair across from the couch he'd chosen. He cradled the glass between his big hands and bowed his head for a moment. When he looked up his eyes were clear and intense.

"I want to apologize for thinking that it was a good idea to get a corporation involved. For not listening when you tried to tell me the cons to go against my pros. We both had valid points, but I believe that in the end I don't want to change the way this works, or put too much red tape on you to do your job. I'm sorry for that."

"Why did you think it was going to be a good idea? Just out of curiosity."

"I honestly thought we could help more boys this way. It's obvious your work is important to you, and I thought doing it for a bigger group might make you happy. But I also started thinking that more kids would mean less one-on-one time and less feeling like a family. That would be contrary to what Crockett wanted." He sighed. "And despite what everyone seems to think, I do want what Crockett wanted for these kids. Coming back here has been a reminder of all the good things, when I've only thought about the bad ones for over half my life."

"I understand, and I appreciate where you were coming from and that you are no longer going there."

He laughed. "My Liv, always so forgiving and quick to take an apology."

She smiled. "Not always. But I do appreciate your coming over here."

"And I appreciate your not bashing in my head when I knocked on the door."

"I'm not that bad."

"No, you're actually very good. Crockett knew what he was doing." He rose from the couch and came over to her. Bending down, he kissed her forehead, and she desperately wanted him to lay his lips just about five inches lower, right on her lips.

He stepped back instead and tucked his hands into his pockets. "I should go."

You should stay. Forever. She kept the thought to herself only by biting her tongue.

"Heading out tomorrow?" she asked instead.

"Everything's done here. I should get back to my regularly scheduled life. But I'll try to come out again. Maybe we can go over some ideas, ones that are in line with what you think is best for this place. And we still need to talk about how to house the boys who will work at Beckham's. We can do that when I come back."

If he came back. Because once he got home, back to his takeout food and his fancy clothes and upscale apartment, this might all feel like a weird side trip, and he might get so busy it faded from his mind until she sent him the monthly update via email.

Now she bit her lip, not to keep the words in but to keep the tears from coming. She had to get him out of here before she broke.

"Well, I'll see you tomorrow. Make sure you say 'bye to the boys before you go. You've been good for them."

"And they've been good for me. Thank you, Liv, for all you do and all you've done. Crockett would be proud. I can't think of a better compliment than that for you."

She could think of a couple of other words she'd rather hear, but instead she smiled and waved him out of the house. She hadn't apologized, but she could do that later. At least she'd be able to sleep now, but when she woke up he'd be leaving and taking a piece of her heart with him without even knowing it.

The rest of that heart was beating so hard she wondered that it didn't pound through the window. She leaned up against the pane with her hand flat on the glass and the words on the tip of her tongue to call him back.

And then he turned around and looked at her. He raised his hand in a goodbye that she felt clear down to her toes. It would never be the same. Never.

Not able to stand the sight of him leaving, she turned around and wrapped her arms around her middle. She'd see him tomorrow and give him a goodbye. She'd see him again when he came back. Things would fall into a routine. She wouldn't dread calling him anymore, and he would stand with her to get things moving in a bigger and better direction. She had never thought it would end up like this when she made that fateful call. Wanting more at this point was just plain selfish.

Until a knock sounded on the door behind her. She'd forgotten to lock it, or just hadn't gotten around to it yet, and Alex came through to wrap his arms around her from behind.

"This is not a good idea. I just want to put that out there before I ask you to come to bed with me. I won't be angry if you say no, but I have to take the chance and ask or never know if I could have had at least one night with you."

She gulped. "No is the very last word on my mind right now, the absolute last."

He laughed and kissed her nose, then zeroed in on her mouth with an intensity that curled her toes.

Paul had been a good husband, but she had never experienced a lover like Alex. He took his time, backing her through her small cottage until her thighs hit the edge of her bed. He slowly took off her shirt, kissing and tasting every single inch he exposed with methodical care.

She nearly wept when he palmed her breast and sealed her lips with his. The sensation, dual pleasures that she hadn't felt in so long, soared through her. Her heart clenched in her chest and her breath shortened when he slid off her panties and kissed her hipbones.

And then he took her to the mattress and entered her with a care that did cause a few tears.

"Am I hurting you?"

"No, God, no, please don't stop."

"As you wish."

She giggled, as that was a line from her favorite movie, then sighed in ecstasy when he started moving. She'd never felt more alive, never more whole, than when she was in his arms.

When it was over, they lay together for long minutes. Her head rested on his chest and his fingers played in her hair.

"I can't ask you to come to DC with me."

"I know."

"And I can't live here, no matter how much I appreciate it now."

She sighed. "I know."

"I should go."

Another couple of tears leaked out of her eyes, but she caught them before they could land on his chest. "I know."

"You're being awfully understanding, when this is ripping me up inside." He shifted and tipped her chin up to look in her eyes.

"I don't know what you want me to say, Alex. This was incredible. You're incredible. But I can't leave and neither can you. I have made my peace with that." She'd made her peace with herself too. There would never be another Alex, but maybe she had shut herself off too completely to anything that wasn't Breathe. She wasn't going to start dating or anything until she could figure out how to get over this amazing man, if ever, but it was a step in the right direction.

Looking at the clock on her bedside table, she winced at the time. Everyone would be up in a few hours. He couldn't be here in her bed.

The whole camp would go wild—with glee and hope, probably. But she wouldn't expose the younger ones to anything that wasn't completely aboveboard.

After rising from the bed, she grabbed a robe and wrapped it tight around her. "I don't want you to go, please know that, but I think it would be best if you woke up in your own bed in the morning."

"Here's your pants, what's you're hurry?"

She'd hurt him, and she hadn't meant to, but looking at him sprawled in her bed was hurting her, and she couldn't do this, knowing he was leaving. It had been a mistake. A glorious one, but a mistake regardless.

Not wanting to fight with him, she didn't answer, just gave him a sad smile and went to the bathroom to collect her pajamas. When she returned, he was gone. It was probably for the best.

Then why did she spend the rest of the night crying into her pillow?

****

Alex was outside at ten in the morning and ready to hit the road. He might not wait as long to come back and visit, but it would be different when he did. Here he had found a peace he hadn't realized he'd been seeking.

But he couldn't stay. He had a life in DC, and Liv had her own life here. He cared for her and wished her well, but at the end of the day he belonged in the city. Obviously she thought the same thing, since she'd kicked him out while the sheets were still warm.

Hugs were exchanged with each of the kids as he stood next to his car. He hoped to see some of these faces, if not all of them, next year and would come back for the first day of camp to welcome them. He hoped it wouldn't be too uncomfortable being that close to Liv and knowing she could never be his, but he'd do it for the boys, if nothing else.

Liv not wanting him would not keep him away. He was stronger than that, and the boys deserved better from him for the first time since he'd been handed Breathe.

Last but not least, Davey came running out of the house and clung to Alex's leg. "Do you have to go?" He looked up with tears in his eyes that almost broke Alex's heart. If Davey's mother had wanted him, he might have tried to make it work, but he knew when he had exceeded his welcome, and the time had definitely come to go.

"Yeah, buddy, I do, but I gave you my cell phone number, so you call me if you need me, okay?"

"Okay." Twin tears slid out of his deep green eyes, so like his mother's. His gaze darted around to see if anyone was watching, and then he dashed the moisture away. "I'll look after Mom while you're gone. We'll make sure this place runs as good as possible. And you won't be sorry that you helped me get my alpacas. I'll make all kinds of money to help the kids that get to stay here and enjoy the summer."

"You do that, and next time I'm here we'll talk investing."

"I'll do research so I know what you're talking about."

Now Alex got a grin from the boy and that was better. At least he could leave feeling marginally not like he was crushing anyone.

He watched over Davey's head to see if Liv would

come out. They hadn't parted on the best of terms last night, but that could be smoothed out once they weren't in each other's pockets anymore. He'd gotten in too deep too quickly. And now he'd leave and think about it later.

She still hadn't come out when he dropped into the seat of his car. Maybe it was best this way.

And then she was there at his window. He rolled it down and smiled at her.

"Safe travels," she said.

"Thanks for everything."

"Sure thing. Door's always open whenever you need a rest from the rat race."

"Well, since I'm one of the rats, I don't know if it's fair to think I get a rest." It was as if nothing had happened last night. If she could act that like, then so could he.

"Aw, you're not a rat. You did good things here. I do appreciate what you tried to offer last night, but I hope you understand that I just can't do it. I'm sorry I pulled your mother into it. It was a gut jab I shouldn't have gone for."

"I do understand you can't do it, and thanks for the apology. I needed to know." He wasn't going to mention that he had spoken to his mother. He needed to process that before he said anything. And he'd rather leave here thinking he did good for the most part.

Just not good enough for her to take a chance on him. He understood. She had her life and he had his, and there wasn't a way to make them meld. He wasn't going to ask her to come to the city. She'd shrivel there. And he wouldn't take Davey away from everything he knew. And as much as he had changed, he just couldn't see himself living out here, not full-time. And Davey needed full-time. So did Liv, and it was something he just couldn't offer.

He started the engine and waved to everyone as he pulled out of the drive. Bill led the boys in a group goodbye wave, and Alex watched them in his rearview mirror every few seconds until he couldn't see them anymore. He'd do everything he could from a distance to help them be the men he knew they could be.

Finally he understood Crockett's love for the place. Life would be different when he got home. He'd no longer just give Breathe lip service to impress people. He'd actively start soliciting donations and perhaps have some kind of program he could set up to bring some of the kids from the streets around where he lived instead of just from Philly and the Harrisburg area.

He'd talk about it with Liv in a couple of weeks, after he'd put some distance between himself and all the things she'd made him feel.

Heading out the way he'd come, he waved to Betty, who stood on the sidewalk in front of Petri's Dish. She waved back and used the tail of her apron to wipe at her face. This time he was choosing to leave on his own, but he knew he'd be welcomed back and was wanted. It was different from being stolen away like last time. And this wasn't the end but maybe a new and different beginning.

Alex was well out of town when his phone rang on the seat next to him. With all the twists and turns to get on the expressway, he wasn't going to try for hands free.

His car radio announced the call was from Breathe just as he came to that stop sign where'd he'd made a wrong turn what seemed like a really long time ago but was only actually a little under a week. He turned around and pulled into the parking lot at Bob's. Hal, with his self-proclaiming hat, waved from the front of the store.

By the time Alex got his phone in hand, the call had gone to voicemail. The voicemail icon popped up, so Alex dialed in his password and listened to Davey's message.

"We have an alpaca emergency. I need you to come back right now. I can't solve this by myself and I need you. Please come back. I think Murray ran away and I don't know how to find him."

"Davey, who are you talking to?" he heard Liv say in the background.

"No one."

"Lying? You know that's not how we operate around here."

Alex sat still as the call was disconnected.

He'd lied to her, too, and he had to go back and make it right. But first, flowers and something that would mean something to her.

Jumping out of his car, he told Hal his dilemma and who it was for, and the guy came through with flying colors.

****

Liv's heart broke. It had been twenty minutes since she'd clicked the off button on the portable house phone, and Davey was still hunched over on the couch, not talking.

"Let's get some lemonade and a few cookies and talk about stuff. We'll go to the cottage. This is just you and me time."

"Okay, Mom." For the first time in a while, Davey reached out and grabbed her hand in front of all the boys who had been at the camp all summer. He was hurting, and she'd have to figure out how to make it better even while she was slowly dying inside. Such was the benefit and the hurt of being a mother.

They sat at the kitchen table where she'd first had Alex in for lunch after he'd messed things up with Beckham, or at least she'd thought he had. But in the end it had turned out better than she could have hoped.

He'd brought her flowers from his father's gardens and had placed them in her hands in an effort to push his way in the door. And that was the beginning of him pushing his way into her heart.

"I lied twice, but I really want Alex to come back, and you didn't make him stay. Why didn't you make him stay, Mom? Do you think he'd come back if I bribed him with my alpacas? He could help me raise them. We'd be partners."

"Baby," she said, "I couldn't ask him to stay because this isn't where he belongs. I'm so happy he finally got to see what his dad always wanted him to see. But he doesn't want to be here all the time. And that's okay."

Davey burst into tears. "But I love him. I want him to stay. I love Uncle Bill, but Alex is different. He's like the kind of person everyone talks about when they talk about their dad."

"Oh, sweetie. I get it. I really do." If he kept this up, she wasn't going to be able to hold back her own tears. "I can't do anything, though. I'm not going to ask him to give up his whole life to be out here away from everything he knows. He would never have asked that of me, and I appreciate it. I have to respect what he wants."

"Did he say he didn't want to stay? Did he come right out and say it when you asked?"

She shook her head, not wanting to lie to him. "We didn't talk about that."

"But you love him, right? I heard you crying like you did when Crockett left, like your heart was broken."

"You are way too observant and too old for your britches. Now come on. Let's go play with the new scanners that just came in for our online drawings of this place. Joaquin is setting them up for us now, and they should be ready to go."

"But wouldn't he stay to love you?"

"I'd like to stay," Alex said from the doorway.

Chapter Sixteen

Liv's heart stopped and then galloped like a runaway alpaca. He was here. Alex was here. How long had he been here, and how much had he heard?

Davey took the opportunity to leave them alone, saying he needed to check on his alpacas. He mouthed the word "bribe" to her on his way out the door, and she shook her head at him. He was a hooligan and her heart.

Part of it, anyway, since the rest was sitting across the table from her. She hadn't realized how much she loved this man until he came back through her door. And now her heart really would break when he left, but at least she'd get to say a real goodbye.

"Why are you here?" Liv asked Alex from across the kitchen table.

"I had to come back. Apparently Murray might have run away." He fiddled with the vase of flowers he'd picked her. The blooms were drooping but still holding on.

Liv sighed. "Davey was lying to you. I'm sorry if you came back for a lie."

"No, I came back to apologize for a lie."

She sat up straighter. "What?"

"I've been thinking about those instances I disappointed you and where we could start over. You mentioned them when I first got here. You know, the ones where you wanted to know where we should have started over again. And they all lead to one thing. A time when you wanted me to help, or stay, or be a part of your life, and every time I left. I didn't always have a choice. I didn't even realize there was a choice to be made. But you did. And I left this time, too, but I didn't know why. This place did have a lot of bad memories for me. You made new ones, and now I don't think I want to leave."

"What do you mean you don't want to leave? You have a life and a townhouse and a business." She had a heart that couldn't handle him being around all the time if they weren't together. And after last night, she'd never be able to look at his hands day after day and not remember how they'd made her moan his name.

"I'm thinking about staying. I could work from here just as easily. You can keep the cottage, of course, but maybe we could put a small apartment over the garage for me. I won't be in your way."

And there was that "in your way" again. Davey had said the same thing. Did she always make people feel like they were a burden?

"I don't think you'll be in my way, and you can do whatever you want. It's your property and your business. If you think living here is a good thing, then go for it." And she would just figure out how to see him and not want him every second of every day.

"Would that be okay with you?"

"Of course." She got up and poured herself a glass of water and one for him. She needed something to do. Davey had asked if he'd stay to love her, and Alex had said he would like to stay. But was that in answer to Davey's question or only a statement that Alex wanted to stay? She didn't have the courage to ask.

"Thanks," he said when she handed him the water. He took a gulp and then put the glass down. "And thank you for helping me make new memories. I hadn't realized how much I missed this place until I came back. All those years I could have had with Crockett..."

He trailed off, and she touched his hand. When he wove his fingers together with hers, she was the one gulping.

"I can't say I understand your bad memories, though I can sympathize. But since this place saved my life, I'm trying." She took her hand back and fiddled with the ends of a placemat Beatrice Smally, from the local craft circle, had made for her. "I only had terrible memories before, and this place was only ever good to me. Uncle Bill brought me and my two sisters here when our mother died in a car accident." She paused and drew in a breath for courage. "An accident caused by the fact that her blood alcohol content was almost four times the legal limit. She hit a tree, and it was over within seconds. The state was going to place us in separate homes or in an orphanage, but Crockett told our uncle to bring us here because no one deserved to go without a home when there was family to take care of them."

"Two totally different takes on one place that can either grow you or stunt you."

She bit her lip to hold back the words she wanted to say. This place wouldn't have stunted him. It would have grown him if his mother had given him a chance to plant roots here. But she hadn't, and Liv was not the one who was going to bring up that topic again. She'd botched it badly at dinner and was lucky she even still had a job after the things she'd said.

"It's not just two takes," she said instead. "Both of my sisters ran as soon as they were old enough to leave." One she hadn't seen in almost seven years, right after Davey had turned one, and the other came back once a year for Christmas and never at any other time. Not even for Davey's birthday. He barely knew the one who did come back and didn't remember the one who'd left at her earliest possible moment.

"That must have hurt."

"It hurts Bill more than me." She shrugged. "I have my life and they have theirs. I can't change what they wanted to do or what they felt they had to do. I needed to stay here and make a life for myself and Davey after Paul died. Crockett and Bill were invaluable in helping me with raising him the best I could as a single parent. Once Crockett died, it was me and Bill, and we're doing okay with the kid." She laughed. "Actually, sometimes I feel like there are a couple too many parents sticking their noses in, but it's better than having no one."

"I don't doubt it. Dad and Bill could be a formidable team when they put their heads together. My mom almost never won an argument when both of them were involved. It drove her crazy. You don't have anything to worry about, though. He's a great kid."

Grabbing a napkin from the basket in the center of the table, she twisted it into a spiral. "I worry, though, and a few things you said make me wonder if I've done the right thing keeping him here."

He darted to kneel on the floor next to her and took one of her hands into his. "You're doing a great job, and he really is a great kid. He has a depth and a heart that I don't think I've seen in anyone since Crockett."

She laughed, then sniffed to keep herself from crying. "Paul wasn't on board with it, but I named our son after Crockett by calling him Davey. He was bigger than life when I was young. I know he wasn't perfect, but after my life on the streets, he was a cushion I needed and a place to land that took care of me. I don't expect you to understand that, but that's how I will always see him."

"Makes sense."

She nodded because she didn't know what to do as she stared into his blue eyes. The lashes fringing them were long and dark. He had the beginnings of crinkles at the corners. From smiling? From squinting? When he'd come here a few days ago, he hadn't laughed much, but he'd started loosening up. At least until last evening, when she'd ruined it.

"I'm sorry for what I said about your mom last night and for ruining dinner. I tend to get very defensive about this place, and I should have thought about your situation before I said those things. I don't know the story and should have kept my mouth shut." Well, at least she'd apologized for real this time, without opening the wound again. She'd planned on saying something to him after he got home, but today was even better.

"Actually, it set things in motion that probably should have been done years ago. My mother admitted that it was less for me than for herself that she took me, and you weren't far off with that gentlemen's farm thing, either. She took me without telling him."

Her heart clenched for him and for the way Crockett had secluded himself. "I remember that day. I wasn't involved, since I had only been here two weeks, but Uncle Bill told us to leave Crockett alone when he didn't come out of his office that whole day."

Alex leaned his forehead against hers. "I had no idea. I thought he wanted me gone. I thought he had told my mom that he wanted us gone. That's what she told me when we left."

When he closed his eyes, she kissed his eyelids and put her hands on either side of his face. "He talked all the time about when you'd come back." She laughed softly. "He thought we'd make a good team."

Opening his eyes, he stared at her, and her heart fluttered like it never had before. "I bet we would have."

"That's in the past." She rose from her chair because being this close to him was too much. When she'd laid her lips on his eyelids, she wanted to kiss him everywhere, to take the hurt and make it go away. To take him with her wherever he wanted to go. To be with him as more than just boss and director.

He might want to stay, but he would never be hers. For one thing, he'd have to open his heart up, and for another, so would she. It was one thing to enjoy his kisses, to let him into her body, and to wish it were different, but real life would intrude, and she couldn't handle being left again when the farm was no longer new or fun.

"But we could start a new future. Couldn't we?" He sat back at the table, watching her walk around the kitchen that felt way too small to her.

"You can absolutely start a new future, and I'm sure the boys will love having you here. They trust you and like you. You're like Crockett in so many ways, but better in others. You bring a sense of wonder to the place that I think I might have lost along the way." She forced herself to smile. Every word was true, but every one hit her hard in the heart. What would it be like to work with him? To have him underfoot but know he wasn't with her? She didn't want to think about it.

But he was here now, and maybe that meant something. She was just too afraid to think it might.

"So then we'll start on construction. Maybe the boys would like to learn how a house is made." He took another sip of his water. "And we can start making plans to bring the boys back for the winter. With me here, decisions can be made faster."

"Email was fast enough," she said.

He set the glass on the table again and clasped his hands together in front of him. "Do you want me to leave, Liv? I know you've been independent for a long time. Having the boss live on the premises probably isn't what you thought you'd be dealing with when you woke up this morning. I'll go if you don't want me here. I don't want to be where I don't belong."

"Bill would be thrilled if you moved back here. Crockett will be crowing in the afterlife. Davey will think all his dreams have come true."

"And you, Liv, what about what you will think if I'm here most of the time?"

He was going to make her say it. And she would because she wanted something for the first time in her life, just for herself, and maybe it was time to finally take a step into the unknown. "I waited for you just like Crockett asked me to, even though I didn't realize I was."

He rose from his chair and wrapped his arms around her waist. Kissing her eyelids and then her cheek and finally her mouth, he delved in deep. She opened for him, knowing that her life was about to change, and she couldn't wait for it.

"I would have come sooner if I had known," he said when they came up for air. "I love you, Liv. I don't know when it happened. But I'm so grateful it did. And I'm going to spend the rest of my life proving it to you."

Tears formed as Davey rushed into the room. "I told you you only needed to ask! I didn't even have to bribe him!"

The three laughed together, and for the first time in a long time Liv looked forward to a future filled with the love of a good man and raising her child with someone who got him and her.

"I love you, too, Alex Campbell."

All the dreams she'd had coalesced into that one moment. She'd jumped in feet first, taken the plunge and stopped playing it safe. And it would pay off in hugs and kisses and love like she hadn't known before.

Life just didn't get better than this.

Bill was going to be insufferable when she told him, but she could handle anything with this wonderful man at her side.

Epilogue

Three months later

It was supposed to be a small affair, just a few friends and her uncle. This was not going to be the wedding of the century. It was Liv's second, after all, and Alex had said he was okay with small and intimate.

Then again, she hadn't counted on him conspiring with Betty. He hadn't actually lied to her about the wedding, since she'd just assumed he was going along with her small plans, but apparently everyone in town had been in on it, and now everyone in town was here. She'd looked out the second-story window earlier, and the sheer number of chairs had started her wondering. When guests started showing up and milling around, it was another notch in the meter of how big this thing was going to be.

And then she'd gone to the widow's walk for a quick breath of fresh air and realized the camp bus was gone, only to watch it turn in the drive from her vantage point.

When it stopped at the front of the house, every boy from the past summer spilled out in ties and nice shirts and pants. The woman who owned the thrift store stepped out last and inspected each of Liv's boys, straightening a tie here and shooting a cuff there. She slicked down hair and gave compliments and pats on the arm. She must have cleared out everything on her racks.

And then there was Bill stepping out of the driver's seat. She'd wondered where he was. He was supposed to be waiting downstairs to walk her down the aisle, but apparently he had picked up the boys from the train station and taken them to get dressed, instead. She'd happily wait until everyone was settled before starting the procession, if it meant everyone she loved was here to witness her giving her heart to the man she loved beyond words.

Her life was so full that tears threatened. Maddie stood at the doorway to the widow's walk. "Get back in here. We have a wedding to put on, and we don't need the groom to see his lovely bride. It's bad luck."

"I don't think bad luck could touch me, with all the amazing things in my life."

"Not bad luck then, but I will say that Bill arranged for a few other unexpected surprises. The one below is good, but the other two might not be. I don't want you to be taken off guard, so I'm just going to tell you that your sisters are here. Everyone will forgive a new mother for blurting that out."

"Yep." Liv hooked her arm into her best friend's. "Sisters will be fine. Bill will be thrilled, and maybe I can get some alone time with my husband. *If* this ceremony ever gets off to a start."

Just then the first strains of music hit Liv's ears. She looked down from three stories up and found Alex looking at her. He blew her a kiss, and she could have gladly floated down to him.

Instead she picked up her skirts and ran down the stairs, Maddie huffing and puffing behind her.

She was ready to start the rest of her life.
Right this very moment.
And it all began with Alex.

A word about the author…

Misty Simon loves a good story and decided one day that she would try her hand at it. Eventually she got it right. There's nothing better in the world than making someone laugh, and she hopes everyone at least snickers in the right places when reading her books.

She lives with her husband, daughter, and three insane dogs in Central Pennsylvania, where she is hard at work on her next novel or three.

She loves to hear from readers, so drop her a line at:

misty@mistysimon.com
www.mistysimon.com

Thank you for purchasing
this publication of The Wild Rose Press, Inc.

For questions or more information
contact us at
info@thewildrosepress.com.

The Wild Rose Press, Inc.
www.thewildrosepress.com

To visit with authors of
The Wild Rose Press, Inc.
join our yahoo loop at
http://groups.yahoo.com/group/thewildrosepress/

www.ingramcontent.com/pod-product-compliance
Lightning Source LLC
Chambersburg PA
CBHW070112260626
47160CB00004B/1431